D1526018

IF YOU SEE KAY RUN

Enjoy the giggle snort

FIONA QUINN

TINA GLASNECK

Fiona Quinn

Powhatan County Public Library
270 Mill Road
Powhatan Va 23139
(804) 598-5670

WITHDRAWN

If You See Kay ...Run is a work of fiction. Names, characters, places, and incidents either are the product of the author's imagination or are used fictitiously, and any resemblance to actual persons, living or dead, business establishments, events, or locales is entirely coincidental.

©2017 Fiona Quinn and Tina Glasneck
All Rights Reserved

Cover created by Chandell Aikman Sites

Publisher's Note:

Neither the publisher nor the authors have any control over and do not assume any responsibility for third-party websites and their content.

No part of this book may be scanned, reproduced, or distributed in any printed or electronic form without the express written permission from the publisher or author. Doing any of these actions via the Internet or in any other way without express written permission from the author is illegal and punishable by law. It is considered piracy. Please purchase only authorized editions. In accordance with the US Copyright Act of 1976, the scanning, uploading, and electronic sharing of any part of this book without the permission of the publisher constitute unlawful piracy and theft of the author's intellectual property. If you would like to use material from the book (other than for review purposes), prior written permission must be obtained by contacting the authors at FionaQuinnBooks@Outlook.com and Tina@TinaGlasneck.com

Thank you for your support of the authors' rights.

For friendship ... that's what it's all about!

CHAPTER 1

MEN JUST DON'T LISTEN when you explain things the first time.

"Why don't you answer the phone when I call?" Officer Peter Harris spun the wheel on his police cruiser and pulled into the park entrance, sliding up into the shade of a tulip tree and turning off his engine. Peter had a dash of old-fashioned convention when it came to our relationship. 'Relationship' should probably be in quotes. It implied the idea of an emotional commitment, and while I liked Peter just fine, at twenty-two with my life just getting started, being in a relationship was pretty far down my to-do list. Either Peter needed to get on the same page that I was reading, or I needed to pick another book from my shelf.

My name is Roberta Jaqueline Reid. My oldest and best friends call me Bobbi Jax, but now I prefer to shorten it down to BJ. In my social life, I had a man code. Everyone who seeks to visit my temple had better be single. I don't do married men, engaged men, or men with girlfriends. Divorced men came with baggage that I didn't want to carry. Nope. My guys needed to be decidedly single and out for a good time. Like I was. They also needed to be fit, and fine. But most of all, they needed to wear a navy-blue uniform and flash their badge at me.

Officer Pete here, with his chatter about getting together for dinner and answering last-calls-of-the-night, was starting to ruin things.

"Peter, I like you a lot, but right now, what I'd really like to do is to put a crease or two into that sharp uniform of yours." I stretched out my bare legs in the passenger side of his police cruiser, let my knees fall just a little bit apart, and slid the full skirt of my flowered dress up my thighs, showing off a swirl of white netting that I knew would move Peter's blood from one head to the other. "I know there are better things you can do with that mouth of yours." I sent him a cupid bow's smile and a flutter of lashes.

Wearing his blue uniform, Peter appeared almost dashing. His black hair neatly trimmed, his youthful square-shaped face with intelligent eyes, and his large hands were all to my liking. Most important, though, was that his left ring finger was bare.

His eyes darkened as he shifted around to make room in his trousers for the standing ovation he was giving me for the show I'd just put on.

"Why don't you tell communications that you're going to investigate what's happening behind those bushes over there?" I tilted my head toward the screen of white azaleas.

Peter reached his hand over, sliding his fingers down my thigh, down my calf to my ankle, then lifted my foot into his lap. Pulling off my high-heeled sandal, he stroked his hands over my arch and played with my toes in their newly-pedicured orchid pink.

He licked his lips as he lifted the radio handset. And with a smile that was sure to be heard by the communications officer, he pressed the button and said he was at Marble Hill Park, and he was getting out to do foot patrol.

See? Badges were my thing. Feet were Peter's. Personally, I didn't get the allure, but who was I to judge?

In the warm Virginia spring day, I pulled myself free from Peter's grasp, tugged off my other shoe, and popped open the door. As I got out, I looked over my shoulder. "Don't forget your hat."

Peter nodded and reached to the hook on the back of the passenger's seat. Pulling it into place, he sent me a raised brow to see if he'd done what I wanted. I smiled and ran barefooted toward the tangle of branches. Pushing the flowers aside, I was pleased to find a lovely little cove that surrounded us like a protective donut. It was a perfect space that seemed to be constructed for just such an afternoon romp. In the middle of the space that was surrounded—I thought rather romantically—by the full blooms, I bent to wriggle my lace panties off as my friend Peter fumbled with his belt buckle.

"I've been polishing my big gun thinking of you," he said in all seriousness.

Why guys named their private parts, I don't think I'll ever understand. But they do. Every single guy I know: the General, Russel the Muscle, the Rock, and of course, Peter's big gun.

When I stood, I slid my undies into my skirt pocket and looked down at Peter's big gun, thinking how much fun it was going to be to polish it myself. I stretched my arm around Peter's neck, pressing myself flat against him. I liked that I needed to stand on my toes to reach him for a kiss. I liked how his biceps bulged against his blue shirt. But mostly, I loved the shiny glow of his badge, pinned there on the left side of his broad chest. "Badge Bunny" is the term used to describe girls like me who get turned on by boys in blue. Yup. Something about that uniform... Woof!

As his lips nipped my neck, I giggled and squirmed with my chin on his shoulder. I held his head in place with my hand.

I opened my eyes and stalled with a gasp.

"I must be doing something right," Peter whispered, and continued tracing kisses down my neck.

"Wait," I said, lowering myself until I was flat-footed and holding onto Peter's arms, then peeked around him to focus on the branches. Sure enough, I saw a woman's eye staring back at me. Some peeping Tom-ess was spying on us. What the heck was wrong with people? Peter tried to move, but since he was waving his flag at full staff, I pinned him in place. I stared the woman down, hoping she'd catch a clue and move on. But no. She just gawked back, unblinking. This was weird.

"What are you doing, baby?"

"I'm nobody's baby," I said reflexively as I pushed around Peter and slunk toward the bush. The woman didn't move. Just gazed back, but now I could see she was smiling.

Alright. I have another line I draw in the sand: To each his own, but it has to be consensual, and I never said this chick could get her jollies watching me get mine. This was perv territory. I moved forward and waved my arms wildly as if to frighten away an animal. Nope. Nada. Not even a blink.

Peter seemed to have figured things out. He was in line to become a detective, so it was good that his mind was working to assess situations and act accordingly. I could sense him shoving his "big gun" back in his holster and zipping himself into place. I was on my knees, pulling the branches apart. If she said anything, I was going to jump out of my skin. This chick was already giving me the shivers.

I put my hand into the foliage, opened a window, and looked in to find another little donut of protection all set up for someone else's tryst. But this one included a mannequin having a picnic. At least, I *thought* it was a mannequin. I reached through the hole and flicked the decidedly feminine cheek. Yep. Mannequin.

"What are you doing?" Peter hunkered over me, his hands balancing on my shoulders. "Huh," he said, which I thought summed up the situation pretty well. And given the fact that he didn't have a lot of blood available for brain function, it was probably the best he could do.

I pulled my panties from my pocket and stepped back into them.

"What are you doing? You're not going to let this stop us, are you?"

I shot him a look of incredulity.

"When you said you liked boys in blue," he gestured toward his crotch, "I didn't think you meant my balls, too."

I stopped to smile—that was actually a pretty good joke, though Peter looked darned serious. I pushed the branches apart and moved into the second little circle of privacy. There was the mannequin, looking as life-like as all get out, with jointed legs that let her sit on a blanket against a tree trunk with her knees pushed up to her chest. Her face turned bashfully to the side as if someone didn't want to be watched while they did the dirty. And dirty they certainly did. The evidence was there on her panties, still a little moist. So, recently.

"Huh," Peter said again. He was turning into the strong silent type, which to be honest is what I preferred.

"Do you need to call backup?" I asked.

"It's a doll," he said.

"This doesn't look odd to you?"

"BJ, in the long list of odd that I see every day, this doesn't even reach my top ten." He ran his hands over my hips and pulled me flush to his big gun.

I was growing annoyed. "Children play in this park."

"We're here to do exactly the same thing this guy did."

He sounded so rational that my irritation grew. Yeah, if he kept this up, he definitely wasn't getting any today. "I'm not plastic, and this is very weird. I think you need to do something about this."

"Like what?"

"I don't know, there's bound to be DNA in that goop there." I gestured toward the periwinkle panties.

He gave me a sexy leer. "I'll give you a DNA sample you can test."

He still hadn't figured out that chapter was done; I'd turned the page. I turned around to face him, crossed my arms over my chest, and tapped my toes on the ground.

His eyes followed down my body, down my leg, all the way to my pretty pink toenails. His face grew red, and he swallowed hard.

I cocked my head to the side, a challenge of some kind. Follow through or we're through. Something like that. I don't know how he read it, but he seemed to get some kind of message.

"What would you have me do? I'm not calling a detective in for a mannequin in the bushes. I care about my career."

I'd read my fair share of police novels—okay, probably more than my fair share. Point being, I'd learned a thing or two about how things worked. That and my best friend Kay was a paralegal, so I got to hear all the behind-the-scenes scuttlebutt.

"How about you write up an incident report, snap some pictures, and take the panties to the evidence room?"

"But why?" He was whining now, which was never a sexy look.

I suddenly got the heebie-jeebies and grabbed at Peter's arm. I lowered my voice until I was barely audible. "What if the perv is still here, watching us? Oh my god, get the mannequin and let's go."

"What do you want me to do with it?" He looked horrified at what I was suggesting.

Okay, here it is. Something about the life-like quality of this mannequin was weirding me out. That it had joints weirded me out even more. If this was a run-of-the-mill department store mannequin that would be one thing. If this was even someone's blow up doll, *meh*. But this looked *so* real. It seemed important. I wasn't going to let this go. So, I manipulated the guy.

"Peter," I cooed, rubbing my hands over my breasts. "Do you know what makes me hot?"

He froze. Yeah, I had his attention.

I swung my hips, making my skirt sway, and licked my bottom lip. "I like to see cops in action. I want to see you pull on a pair of gloves and gather evidence." I squeezed my elbows close together to make the girls pop up over the edge of my pretty little sundress.

Peter was sweating.

I blinked at him.

He ran toward his car. "I'll be right back. I just need to get an evidence kit. Don't go anywhere."

"I wouldn't dream of it."

CHAPTER 2

Peter wasn't happy with me, and I really didn't like that. I'm not a tease. I didn't like it when girls revved a guy's engines up for no reason. But these were special circumstances. It wasn't every day that I came across anything like the mannequin situation. Also, it took Peter some time getting things done properly at the scene. He'd called park maintenance and gave them the GPS coordinates for our azalea getaway. They said they'd send a crew over in the morning to clean it all up. That meant dump everything in the trash bins, and that felt wrong. She was so human-looking. So friend-of-a-friend. She felt familiar. *She.* Ha! I was referring to the mannequin as if it were human. And you don't throw people away.

By the time Peter got that all straightened out, it was time for me to head in to work. Hooch had asked me to come in early to the bar for a meeting.

All the way through town as I headed toward Hooch's, something about that mannequin scraped at me. I was sure this went beyond a "perv takes a doll on a date" thing. But what, I had no clue.

I was trying out different scenarios in my head when I pushed my way into Hooch's bar. Hooch was my dad's best friend and fishing buddy, and had been like a second dad to me since I was born. He treated me like the son he'd never had. My dad did, too, for that matter. There were no princesses in my house growing up. Mom took off with a used car salesman or something equally slimy when I was around three years old, and Dad and Hooch had raised me the only way they knew how. That's why I knew my way around an engine and could spit a loogie better than most of the men in my dad's fire department, and it's probably why I had what most would consider a male moral code when it came to sex.

Hooch wasn't just family, and he wasn't just my boss, he was my saving grace. When I graduated from college last year with a business degree, I landed an entry level job at a Fortune 500 company, I was on my way! Out the door. Nope. I couldn't do it. I could *not* claw my way up a corporate ladder. And the idea of wearing pantyhose for the next thirty years made me almost suicidal.

I was there in Hooch's drowning my sorrows in my beer one night when Hooch told me he had his own problems. A bar around the corner was now pulling the cop crowd, and he was losing business, big time. Hooch's bar was literally one block east of the police department, and everyone knew that cops drank like fish. Hmm, fish probably didn't need to drink. Well, cops drank a lot. A *lot*. His property should be gold.

I suggested that Hooch try to win them over by making his own brand of alcohol that honored the hard-working officers. That was the night that Badge Bunny Booze became Hooch's house label. Yeah, he knew what I was up to in my social life, and it was all cool with Hooch. I suggested

"Badge Bunny Booze" might be sexist, because it didn't include the women on the force. Hooch scoffed, "Lot you know," and off he went to design the label. That was also the night that I got the gig as his manager. Whoop! The next day, I resigned from my Fortune 500 nightmare, and left my pantyhose in the trash on my way out. I'd been working here at Hooch's for almost a year now and felt right at home.

Home enough, anyway, that I could make my way through the bar while my eyes adjusted to the low lighting. I saw Hooch sitting on a stool in his typical Hawaiian shirt, baggy cargo shorts, and flip-flops. What was new was the suitcase sitting by his feet.

"Heading out?" I asked, sitting next to him.

"Yep," he said.

A file folder was open in front of him with a blue pen resting on top. I looked to our right—a little weasel-looking guy sat in the booth, wearing a dark blue suit and very shiny shoes on his dainty little feet. I rolled my lips in and waited.

"I'm going to take a trip. A sabbatical, if you will."

"Okay," I said, knowing that was the opening pitch, and the game would soon follow.

"I have a proposal. Hooch's, as you know, is having trouble. We're headed down the drain. The doc says I need to let go of stress. I need to go hang out on a beach somewhere and watch the waves."

"And the girls in bikinis."

"There is that." He grinned. "I decided, though, not to sell Hooch's. What I'm doing instead is giving you a shot at it."

I tilted my head, not sure where this was heading.

"That's Barney." Hooch lifted his chin toward the weasel. "He's here to notarize this contract." He tapped his middle finger onto the manila folder resting on the bar between us. "It basically says that if you can turn the bar around and make it solvent, then you become my partner. Fifty-fifty. If you fail, and it goes bankrupt, you're the manager, so you're not beholden to any creditors, and I? I'll be off on some island with bikini clad women, so it'll be tough to come after me."

"You're serious?" This day just kept getting weirder and weirder.

"Totally."

I opened the file and read it over. Yep. If the bar became the gold mine it had the potential to be, I got half-stake. If I failed, I'd be none the worse for wear. "You have enough money to live on?" I asked.

"In spades. I'm set for life. This was supposed to be for fun. It's not fun anymore. It's just a drag. And the doc—he says to get rid of the stressors."

I sent a worried eye toward Hooch. "Why did you go see the doctor? What's going on? Is it your heart?"

"It's just old age."

"You're sixty. You're a spring chicken."

"Okay, it was me looking for an excuse to get the hell out of Dodge and chase girls in grass skirts."

That seemed reasonable. I picked up the pen. "When are you leaving?" I asked as the weasel ran over to watch me scrawl my signature onto the contract.

"Plane takes off at five--just in time for opening tonight. There's one catch, though, Bobbie Jax." He put his hand on my arm. "Whatever happens, that prick next door, Nicky, is not—and I mean *not*!—to get this place. He's been trying to run me out of here for years, and I have some pride."

I knew Hooch had been having a pissing contest with the restauranteur next door, Nicky Stromboli, the owner of

"Nicky's." What kind of person was vain enough to name the restaurant after himself, as well as every darned thing on the menu? What the heck is Spaghetti alla Nicky or Caprese alla Nicky? And who wants to eat a Stromboli alla Stromboli? That seems cannibalistic on some level. To me, it read as an egotistical proclamation that Nicky was setting the standard and others could only hope to taste as good. That was self-delusion.

I ate there. Once. It was convenient. I was hungry. The food was subpar at best. He had nice flowers on the tables, though. After that, I made sure to keep a couple menus from restaurants that would deliver next to the phone.

On the surface, you'd think Hooch did the exact same thing as Nicky in naming his place Hooch's. But that is one of those which came first the chicken or the egg discussions. I know the truth. James Bradley, AKA Hooch Bradley, bought a bar already named Hooch's. Well, 'bought' was a stretch. He won it in a poker game. And when he took the reins into his own hands, the long-time customers simply started calling the new owner the old owner's name. It made the transition simpler for their alcohol-soaked brains.

I scowled at Hooch, wondering why Nicky Stromboli would want him out of business. It didn't make much sense to me. You'd think a bar and a restaurant would be kind of symbiotic. "I don't understand."

"Nicky wants to expand into the bar so he has control of the entire block. Of course, that could solve a lot of my problems, but I won't sell to him. If you can't right this ship, I need you to at least make sure it doesn't get into that guy's hands."

I nodded. Hooch had built this place up for the fun of it, and this guy would tear it all down. In the sum of things, we are only what we left behind and the memories we take with us. "I promise, Hooch," I said. I meant and felt each letter of my pledge.

Hooch leaned over and placed a fatherly kiss on my forehead. A stamp of approval, just like he did all my life, from the first time I did a wheelie on my bike to the time I'd knocked back my first double Scotch and didn't mind the burn. He didn't give out that level of praise often, but when he did, it felt like magic.

I watched emotions play behind those wise gray eyes. The weasel interrupted our father-daughter moment when he banged his stamp on the page and entered his numbers. He slid the contract back to Hooch. Hooch stood and with one last "Whoop!", grabbed hold of his duffel, and headed off to Mai Tais on some faraway beach. And for one brief moment I thought, what the hell had I just signed up for?

CHAPTER 3

THAT NIGHT, Hooch's had been kind of slow. That was a bad sign. I knew our clientele had been falling off, but it seemed much more significant now. If I succeeded in turning this place around, I'd be set as far as my career went. If I failed, I'd be back in a pair of pantyhose. Just that thought alone made me desperate for success.

My best friends the Fitzgeralds—Connor and his sister Kay—had shown up to help me celebrate and help me out if I was short-handed. "Speaking of short-handed, Kay, I have a really big favor to ask."

Kay looked up with a slice of orange garnish in her hand. She nibbled out the center, waiting for me to finish.

"I was hoping you would help out here at the bar." I held up a hand to stop her from saying no straight-out. "I know you're busy at work, but this would be some part-time cash, and it would be for a very short time. Just until I can hire some help. It's just me and the dishwasher, Joe, now that Hooch took off. Of course, if things stay this slow, I won't be needing to hire any help." I grimaced.

Kay picked up another slice of orange and seemed to

deeply contemplate the act of peeling the rind from the fruit, then she stuck it in her mouth, chewing slowly, swallowing slowly, smiling slowly. "Okay, I'll do it."

I looked over at Connor. He didn't even wait; he shook his head. "I signed a contract that says I can't take any other jobs. I'm glad to run in and sling some steins if things get really tight, but it would be a friendship thing, not a work-for-you thing."

That was fair. Connor was a sergeant on the police force, and before anyone asks, no, I'd never slept with him. He was darned good looking, and I'm sure one *hell* of a roll. But one, I had real feelings for the man. He was a dear friend. And two, he had a long-standing girlfriend, Ashley. They'd been together ever since high school, as a matter of fact. I didn't get along with her that well—I seldom do with people who sport resting bitch faces as their go to expressions—besides I've got my girl code to follow.

Connor's phone rang, and he swept his finger across the screen. I knew it was Ashley Virginia Randolph by the way he wrinkled his nose before he answered. I wondered if he knew he did that. Sort of like he was smelling B.O. Connor moved away to talk her down from whatever window ledge she was hanging from this time. In the distance, thunder rolled.

"It's going to rain," I told Kay, looking out the big picture window at the moonless night.

"Sounds like it."

I turned to catch her eye. "The mannequin is going to be destroyed."

"They're going to pitch it into the bin tomorrow anyway."

I sniffed. "Feels wrong."

Kay studied me. "Yeah? You're serious?"

"I am. It feels wrong to leave her out there like that in the rain. I think we should go rescue her."

"You understand she's inanimate."

"Which is good since I have boxes in the back of my Mini, and I'll have to tie her to the roof of my car. That is, *if* you're coming."

"If?" she asked.

That right there is why I love Kay.

I closed up the bar early. Shit, I was in charge. I had no customers. I could do what I wanted to. Connor had to go home and soothe the ruffled feathers of the prima donna, anyway. Kay and I grabbed a pair of plastic food-prep gloves, a couple of garbage bags, and a roll of duct tape. Hooch hadn't really equipped the bar with good mannequin-rescuing tools.

Off we went, with a quick stop by my apartment to fetch my dog Twinkles. I mean, it was one thing to go rescue a mannequin alone in the park with a storm brewing, but it was quite another to do it knowing the perv might be trying to do the same. Twinkles was a must.

Twinkles was my hundred-and-thirty pound, muscle bound, all-male Rottweiler. He got his name because he was a Christmas gift from my dad. I left him alone for two seconds. Two seconds! And he must have eaten a string of twinkling Christmas lights off my little table top tree, battery case and all. I figured this out the next day when he was moaning at the door. I put him on his leash and led him to the dog park so he could do his business and meet some of the neighborhood dogs, maybe make a new friend or two. Everyone was super impressed when he finally made his poop, and it came out with flashing mini Christmas lights. At that point, he kind of got the name whether I liked it or not. So "Thor" went by the wayside, and Twinkles it was. It's okay, he was comfortable in his manhood despite the ridiculous name.

As I loaded us into my car, I looked up at the ominous clouds overhead. In the distance I could see a flash of lightning. Twinkles wasn't a fan of thunder. Let me rephrase that—*I* wasn't a fan of Twinkles and thunder. Something about the low vibrations made Twinkles puke. I usually tried to keep him next to a towel and plastic bag during a thunderstorm, but this was an emergency. Hopefully we'd be home before this became a problem.

When we reached the tulip tree with the azaleas off to the right, Kay gave me a look. "Seriously? You were going to do it here, in the middle of the day?"

"What could go wrong?"

Kay laughed and climbed out of the car. I had Twinkles on a lead, so Kay carried our gear. We snuck into the bushes, and I used the flashlight on my phone to find the mannequin. "She needs a name," I said, aiming my light over to where Peter and I had left her. We had straightened her out and pulled down her skirt for modesty's sake since Peter had packaged her undies. Twinkles let out a menacing growl, then sniffed the mannequin all over.

"Well, she's a redhead. How about Lucy?" Kay offered as she held out a pair of food prep gloves to me.

"Mmm, she's dressed more like Jessica Rabbit," I observed as I pulled the plastic gloves into place.

"Jessica it is. So, what's the plan?"

"I think we should put her in the plastic bag in case it starts raining and tighten it into place with the duct tape. I grabbed some twine when I was getting Twinkles. We can tie her to my roof and drive her back to the bar."

"The bar?" Kay mumbled, then used her teeth to bite off a length of duct tape, and wrapped it around the plastic bag at the mannequin's neck to hold it in place.

"I don't have room for her in my apartment. I think she might be a conversation piece in the bar. Besides, if I get a talker, and he's drunk enough, I'll just push Jessica over to his side to keep him company."

"Sounds like a plan."

And that's what we did.

The trash bags only covered Jessica down to her knees, so her feet were sticking out of the bottom. It turned out the roof of my car was only but so long, so it was a good thing that she had joints in her hips and knees. I could sort of bend her so she was draping, wide-legged, over my back window. She was pretty secure. I looked up at the swirling black clouds and hoped the rain would hold off for a bit. I loaded Twinkles into the car, Kay climbed in, and I cranked the engine.

CHAPTER 4

WE WERE MAKING PRETTY good time through the city when I saw the red and blue lights in my rearview mirror.

Now, don't get me wrong, I get as excited as any girl would when she knows she's about to get up close and personal with a cop. But this time, I was kind of transporting stolen goods. I mean, Jessica didn't really belong to me. Even though I thought there was a nine-tenths rule and maybe something about the spoils of war that might have me covered.

You can't imagine my relief when I recognized the swagger of one Peter Harris, shaking his head and moving up to my window. I rolled the glass all the way down. "Top of the morning to you, officer." I batted my eyelashes and sent him a smile. "I thought you'd be done with your shift by now."

"I got caught up in a B and E. I'm late getting off. I was driving back to the station when what do I hear over the radio?"

I opened my eyes as wide and innocent as I could make them.

"Two females and a big-ass dog are driving down Main Street with a woman tied to the roof of their car, her legs dangling off the back." He raised his eyebrows at me. "And I thought to myself, now, who could that possibly be?"

"Peter, can I just say sarcasm is never sexy?" Twinkles was trying to climb into the front seat so he could sniff Peter, and I was trying to push my dog back. I wasn't having much success. He outweighed me and wasn't nearly as polite. I grabbed my steering wheel and stuck my elbow out to make a barricade. "Look, I know things didn't work out the way we thought they would today. That's not really my fault. But," I worked to explain as I struggled against Twinkles's enthusiastic tongue licks, "I told you I'd make it up to you. And I will."

Kay's laughter as she pressed up against her door caught Peter's attention.

"Hi, Kay."

"Hey there, Peter. I heard that you had an uncomfortable afternoon. I hope you got your color back to normal," she said in all seriousness.

I reached under Twinkles so I could swat her. I didn't need her egging things on in just that moment. I wasn't sure of the laws about this particular situation, but it felt like thin ice to me.

"Do you want to come back to the bar to look for fingerprints on Jessica?"

Peter scrunched his brow. "Jessica?"

I pointed toward the roof. "Maybe after you punch the clock back at the station, you could come by the bar and punch my clock, so to speak?"

"Eww," Kay said, and I swatted her again.

"I'd love to help out dusting for fingerprints, but I don't know how to do that, and I haven't got that kind of equipment. I can make it back to the bar, though. I'll be happy to show you what equipment I do have."

I looked over at Kay. "Who do we know..."

"Richard Bishop?" she offered, holding down Twinkles's bottom so he wasn't shaking it in her face.

"You mean, Dick? You're right! He just got promoted to detective. Yes, I need Dick. And I know he has graveyard shift this week. Let's call him." I turned back to Peter, who was looking like I'd just stolen his favorite toy. "I'm sorry, Peter," I said in all sincerity, putting my hand on his. "Let's—"

The thunder rumbled, and Twinkles's stomach gurgled. He whined pitifully, and I let him lunge toward the window as he gagged up his dinner, some grass, and a whole lot of mucous goo.

Peter engaged his cop reflexes, skipping back out of the way as the spew dripped to the road. He was well-versed from his time as a traffic cop, jumping back from nervous DUI stops.

"Hmm," I said, looking at the flecks that sprinkled his pants and shiny black shoes. "That's kind of a mood killer, isn't it?" I was feeling a little green myself. "How about you send me the dry-cleaning bill, and we try to hook up later this week?"

Peter rolled his eyes, tapped the roof of my car, and sauntered back to his vehicle.

As I started up the engine, Kay sang, "Don't it make his blue balls, don't it make his blue balls, don't it make his blue balls blue-oo?"

Peter turned onto State Street and I was aimed for Hooch's when a whoosh and a buzz muffled Kay's song. Black filled my rearview mirror. "What the heck?" I threw my arm over the back of Kay's seat and looked between Jessica's dangling legs. "What is that?"

"Eyes on the road!" Kay slapped at me. "What are you doing? Put your eyes on the road!"

I jerked the wheel to the right and just missed the center meridian as I swerved to get control. I caught a glimpse of the thing in my side mirror. "Is that a drone?"

Kay turned around backwards in her seat, the seat belt holding her at a weird angle. "It's a drone," she said.

"Hang on, Twinkles!" I turned a sharp right between two high-rises. The noise lessened. "Whew, I thought it was chasing us."

Kay swiveled around in her seat and adjusted her belt. "So did—"

The noise buzzed at my back window again.

"It's back." Kay turned to get a better look.

"Do you think it's the pervert chasing Jessica?" Twinkles was barking his head off at the drone, and I had to scream over him to be heard.

"I don't know. Could be some jerk messing with you."

"Some jerk?"

"Okay, some hulking low-life creep is messing with you. Better?"

"Shut up," I said, taking a left so tight I thought I was going to come up on two tires. It would be great if I could get the person to pilot the damned thing into the side of a building. Left. Right. Right. Left. I was getting dizzy. Ah! Up ahead I saw a parking garage. It wouldn't follow me in there. Surely that would be too difficult to navigate, what with the low ceilings and hairpin turns.

It followed me in anyway.

"Do something!" I screamed at Kay. I worked at following the curving path up to the top of the garage and back down again. My little Mini Cooper, which I bought because I wanted to call it my mini-copper, was shrieking right along with me.

Kay had braced herself with both hands on the door handle and her foot up on the glove compartment. "What the heck am I supposed to do?" She hollered over the tire sounds and buzz of the drone.

"Call someone! Call Dick. Call Peter."

"And tell them what?"

"We're being attacked!" I was on the ground level, and the attendant was leaning out of the booth, watching. I was almost there. I pressed the automatic window and as soon as there was a crack visible, I yelled, "Open the gate! Help! Open the gate!" As the window lowered more, I waved my arm out of the opening. I was *not* going to slow down. I was willing to break right through. I desperately hoped my Mini Cooper had the power to break right through. I watched as the attendant scrambled back into her booth to press a button that lifted the automatic arm.

"Why am I scared of this thing?" I asked Kay as I popped over the lip of cement and powered back out onto the road. "What could that little hunk of plastic possibly do to us?"

Kay pulled her phone out. "Googling," she said as I let the thing chase me down Main Street, heading toward the police department, where I planned to blare my horn and circle the parking lot until someone came out to help us.

"Well, in this YouTube video, the guy retrofitted his drone with automatic rifles, and he can shoot them remotely."

Fear washed over me. I reached out and grabbed her wrist. "Are you shitting me?"

"And this one says they can carry explosives that they

drop, and those too can explode remotely. And this one here says—"

"Stop. Stop. I can't go to the police station and put the officers in danger. We need a plan B. Turn and look—can you see rifles tied on that thing?"

"I am not turning and looking. Do you think I want to get shot in the face by the drone from hell? No."

My phone rang. "Get it, Kay! It might be Dick. He might have an idea."

She opened my phone. "Thank God, Connor!" she yelled into the speaker phone.

"What are you doing? Are you with Bobbi Jax?" Connor asked.

"We're being chase by a drone. What do we do?"

"What?" Connor asked. "Are you playing video games?"

"We're driving down damned Main Street with a damned drone on our ass. Stop asking stupid questions and tell me what the heck to do."

I gave her a quick glance. "The hospital has an underground parking garage. I can never get a cell phone signal down there. I'm heading to St. Esmerelda's."

"Is that Bobbi Jax? You aren't kidding me? A drone is chasing you?" Connor sounded his usual befuddled self when Kay and I got ourselves into predicaments he could never have imagined.

Kay and I screamed "YES!" at the same time as I took a hard left. Another hard left, then we slid into the parking garage.

"Why in the... how in the..."

"Connor?" Kay yelled. "Connor, are you there?" Kay looked at me. "No signal."

I looked in the rearview mirror. "And no more drone."

We high fived. I took a second to fluff my clothes and push my damp hair out of my face. I was sweating like I'd just run a mile on a hot summer's day.

Twinkles had his tongue hanging out and smile on his face. I'd swear he was laughing at us.

"Do you think we need to wait here long?" Kay looked around anxiously. "I don't like that I can't use the phone. I mean, if the perv showed up, we can't get any help."

"We have Twinkles."

"Fat lot of good he'll do if the perv has a gun."

"Let's go out the south exit, and see if we lost him. If we haven't, we'll call Connor for backup and head underground again."

⸻

The ride back to the bar was anticlimactic, which was good, since I badly needed to pee. I wasn't sure my bladder could handle another shot of drone-induced fear.

"I can't believe we got chased by a drone. Have you ever heard of that happening?" Kay asked.

"I don't even know anyone who owns a drone. Who plays with drones? Pimple faced teens who got them for Christmas is my guess. Maybe it was just some bored high schoolers trying to see up Jessica's dress as the wind made it flap around. She isn't wearing any panties, after all."

Kay snickered as she helped me untie Jessica from the roof. We were parked in Hooch's back alley while Twinkles stood guard. Jessica was heavier than she looked. She probably weighed less than I did, but this was dead weight. When I thought the word "dead," a shiver wracked my body. Kay sent me a questioning look.

"I don't know, something about Jessica is giving me the creeps," I said.

"Probably that it's so life-like, and you gave it a name. Maybe we should just dump it in the trash bin and call it a done deal. This is starting to feel like bad juju to me."

"Could you dump Jessica in the bin?" I asked.

Kay took a moment to stare the mannequin in her glass eyes. "No, you're right. There's something kind of odd about this whole scene. And besides, I do think you're onto something in making her the bar's mascot." One block over, an engine revved. "When are you expecting Dick?"

"He said as soon as he can get himself freed up. Who knows what that means?"

"I'm taking off when he gets here. I have work tomorrow, and you probably want some privacy."

"Dick's a detective now. He wears a suit instead of a uniform."

"He still has a badge," Kay offered.

"Meh," I said.

She laughed as she grabbed hold of Jessica's legs and helped me heft her into the back room. "Dick's going to be sad to hear he's not on your playlist any more. Did you tell him that before he offered to come and dust for prints?"

CHAPTER 5

I LOCKED my car and closed the back door to the bar. I leaned against it to catch my breath and brush the wet strands of my long blond hair from my face. "Whew! That storm is really kicking up. I'm glad we got her in before the deluge," I said, shaking myself off and holding up a plastic shopping bag. "Ta da!"

"What's in there?" Kay took it from my hand and opened it up. "A dress, a pair of sandals and some panties?"

"She's bare assed, which I think is a health violation. And the ball gown is a little over the top for Hooch's. I was going to grab a pair of jeans and a cute little top, only Jessica's butt is smaller than mine. I opted for a sundress for her."

"You're insane."

"That goes without saying." I glanced through the doorway as a set of headlights swept across the front. "That must be Dick." I hustled to let him in. He jogged to the door without an umbrella, and I handed him the bar towel I'd snagged on the way over.

"Hey, cutie." He bent down and gave me a quick kiss on the lips.

"Hey yourself. It was nice of you to come over. I kind of feel like Daphne on Scooby Doo. A meddling kid sticking my nose in somebody's business." I laughed.

"Wait a minute," Kay yelled. "That would make me Velma, and I am *not* Velma."

"Who does that make me?" Dick rubbed the towel over his tightly cropped hair. "I'm hoping for Scooby, so I can get a snack later." He wriggled his brows suggestively.

"I think you're going to have to be the walk-on in this scene. Did you bring your fingerprint kit?"

He held it up.

"You know," Kay said with her arm around the mannequin, holding her up. "Once you change the dress on this thing, it's not going to look like Jessica Rabbit anymore. I'm thinking she looks more like a Daphne. The name Daphne has a sisterly quality to it, don't you think? A mannequin you could spill your guts to and trust that it would stay a secret?"

"I get what you're saying." I studied the mannequin and tried out the name in in my head. "Yeah, I think I like that. Okay, Daphne it is."

Dick squinted at the mannequin. "Is this what you want fingerprinted? Are you serious?"

"Yup." I held up my hands. "We've had gloves on the whole time. I don't think we messed anything up. I hope not, anyway."

Dick moved closer. "Hey, dollface," he said with a wink, then turned back to me. "She's kind of cute. I could see why someone might take this thing on a picnic in the park for a little nookie. No problems with pregnancy. No problems with too much chatter. No problems with having your skills compared to the last guy who took a ride."

"I hear your skills are incomparable." Kay said with a blinking, innocent-eyed gaze. "No issues for you there."

I swatted her with a towel.

Dick turned pink and ducked his head to hide his grin.

"And on that happy note," Kay said, "it looks like the rain is taking a break. I need to head home." She kissed me on the cheek, then turned to give a wave. "Bye, Dick."

"*Richard,*" he enunciated slowly as she opened the door.

"To be honest," I said, catching hold of Twinkles's collar, "I really like Dick." I watched the pink in his cheeks deepen to red. He got that confused glassy look in his eyes that told me all his blood had suddenly rushed south, leaving him a little dizzy. His blood needed to do a U-turn. He was just here for some fingerprints. I followed Kay to the front door with Twinkles by my side. Twinkles and I stood under the dripping awning, making sure Kay was safe until she motored out of view.

When I came back in and locked the door, Dick said, "Okay, BJ, tell me what we've got going on here."

"I don't know. A bad feeling in the pit of my stomach? A weird little tingle in my spine. Look at this thing. It looks like it could animate at any moment. I've never seen a mannequin this life-like. And someone left it in the bushes."

"And just what were you doing in the bushes to find it?"

I smiled by way of response. "As it turns out, not much of anything. I did bring the doll to Peter Harris's attention, though."

"He happened to be nearby?"

"He was in the neighborhood," I said vaguely. "He wrote an incident report and took the damp panties, but he said he didn't know how to dust for fingerprints, and so I thought of you."

"Nice that that's why you thought to give me a call." He leaned an elbow onto the bar. "It's been a while, BJ. I thought we were *special* friends."

"We are friends. The *special* kind of stopped when you started wearing a suit." I gave him a little pout.

"I kept my uniform," he said with a smile. "I have it at my apartment. I wouldn't mind keeping it in the trunk of my car, you know, if you ever needed me to change my clothes."

I ran a hand down his arm. "That feels a little like cosplay, doesn't it? I like the real deal. I'm so proud of you for moving up to detective. I bet there's a bevy of girls who will find that sexy as hell."

Dick let out a sad sigh. "Okay, I get it. I'm here for the fingerprints. I guess I'm glad to give you a hand in your little adventure. But let's get the show on the road, so I can move on to *actual* crimes."

I watched Dick do his thing. He kneeled on a towel while he brushed the surface of the mannequin with his powder, lifted the prints with the tape, made cards. Took photographs. He had taken off his suit jacket and was in a pressed white shirt with his tie held in place with a clip. He was focused and very professional. I had to admit, it was getting my blood humming a little bit. Maybe I needed to widen my spectrum of potential dates to include detectives. I'd think about it, anyway. Right now, I was watching a little scowl form between his brows.

"Are you willing to share that thought?"

"It's interesting," he said, and rocked back on his heels. "There are only two sets of fingerprints on this doll. I thought I'd be finding so many that it wouldn't make any sense to try to collect them. I thought I'd be dusting this thing and telling you there was a stew of evidence, and we wouldn't get a good result. But as far as I can tell, there are only two sets."

"That means only two people have had contact with this mannequin?"

"Not necessarily. It could mean that it was washed down, and since that point, only two people have touched it." He pulled out another card and picked up his tape. "It's also interesting that one set seems to cover the whole body and the other set only seems to be on the arms, like the person was carrying it and on the legs where he—I'm saying 'he' because you said you saw ejaculate—would position it if the legs were bent."

"That's how we—I... that's how I found it in the bushes, and I went to investigate, and there she was, up against a tree with her knees bent to her chest to make her nether regions accessible."

"Are her nether regions accessible?" Dick asked, and bent the doll's knee so he could look between her legs. "No, this isn't anatomically correct. Which is meaningful."

"It's meaningful because this thing wasn't made for sexual adventuring?"

"Exactly. Whoever designed this – despite the fact that I wouldn't be all that shocked if this thing suddenly came to life and smacked me for looking between her legs without permission—was doing it to make it look lifelike. It's like one of those Madame Toussaud's wax figures. But it wasn't so he could have a screw buddy." He flicked the mannequin's thigh. "And it's hard. You'd think if he wanted it for a personal relationship, he'd make it out of a different kind of material." Dick started to close up his kit.

"Whoever it belongs to, I think they might want her back."

"How would you know that?" Dick asked.

"Well I wouldn't. I might be conflating two very different weirdnesses."

Dick squinted at me. "You had two 'weirdnesses' today?"

"Well, tonight was the second." I went on to tell him about being chased by the drone.

"You've got me there, BJ. I've never heard of anyone being chased around the city with a drone before, with or without a mannequin strapped to the roof of their car."

"Why do you think that someone left it in the woods?"

"My guess is that you and Peter surprised the hell out of someone. They saw the cop car, and they took off running. They planned to go back for it, probably after dark, but you beat them to it."

Okay, so he knew I was playing in the bushes with Peter. That kind of connecting-the-dots thinking was why he got promoted to detective.

"Just tell me that I'm not the only one hurting tonight because you're playing with dolls."

"You are not the only one who might be feeling a little frustrated. But I sure do appreciate your doing this for me." I kissed him on the cheek with the sisterly kind of peck that seemed to send the right message, because he offered up a sigh with his frown. Poor boy.

CHAPTER 6

I DRAGGED my butt out of bed because Twinkles was whining at the door. I yanked a pair of yoga pants on under the t-shirt I slept in and grabbed Twinkles's lead. I felt creaky and worn out. I was getting too old to stay up all night and still function the next day. I scraped my hair back into a ponytail, thinking what a sad, sad thought that was. I needed to get Twinkles on a different sleep schedule. I grabbed my phone and headed to the dog park.

Sitting on the picnic table, I leaned my head back to soak up some sun. I wasn't a tanning kind of girl—I got bored lying out there on a towel, trying to spit-roast myself into a golden goddess. But a little vitamin D never hurt. And to be honest, with my English lineage, golden goddess divine was never going to happen. The best I could ever hope for was a healthy-looking pink glow. Timing was everything, a couple of minutes too long under the sun and I could be mistaken for a boiled lobster.

As I relaxed back on my elbows and lifted my face to the warmth, my mind was back on Dick and what he said about the mannequin. It didn't really add up. I had done a

Google search last night and I didn't find anything like this quality of mannequin online. Dick had helped me look for a manufacturer's mark, but we found none. It seemed Daphne was a one-of-a-kind mannequin. Dick said it wasn't intended as a sex toy – and I'm assuming he'd know, since he'd worked in Vice before.

Why would someone take a non-sex doll to the park for sex? That seemed like something you'd do in the privacy of your own home. Though, yeah, there was something kind of dangerous and exciting about doing *it* in a public space with the chance of getting caught.

Before those thoughts went any further, my phone buzzed.

"Hey there," I said to Kay. "Are you at work?"

"Yeppers. I had to drink an entire pot of coffee this morning and spike my system into a doughnut-ingested sugar high. But I'm here."

"Thanks for keeping me company last night."

"Are you kidding? I wouldn't have missed it. Hey, listen. The boss is headed over to the police station. They just brought a couple paddy wagons in; we heard about it on the police scanner. They're trying to pick up some new clients."

"I thought lawyers chased ambulances, not paddy wagons."

"That depends on your specialty. The lawyers here at Dewey, Cheatham, and Howe are looking for some lugheads who look like easy money."

"It's good that Mr. Cheatham and Mr. Markley aren't hearing you call them that. Are you sure they don't have a nanny cam up somewhere?"

"Are you kidding? That's what they call *themselves*. They think it's a hoot. Anyway, I was wondering when you're headed to the bar. There's a funny smell in the building today and it's making me wheeze. I thought I'd just go work at one of your tables. That way I'm not too far from the office if I'm needed, but I can reduce my chances of lung cancer."

"Let me jump in the shower, and I'll head right over. I need to get you a key and the code for the alarm system— that way you can go over whenever you need to. Give me forty minutes, okay?"

"Yup, I'll pick us up some lunch for us, and I'll meet you over there."

Kay was leaning against the wall under the awning when I pulled up to Hooch's, exactly forty minutes later. Twinkles had decided he wanted to come in to work with me. As soon as I opened my car door, he squirmed from the back seat to the front, over my lap and over to Kay. *Sure, go on ahead. No need to wait for me to open your door.* I took Twinkles to obedience training once, but everyone else there had little teeny dogs - terriers, Dachshunds, and toy poodles. When Twinkles walked into the ring, everyone got nervous. Twinkles because the other dogs were yipping under his paws and he wasn't sure how to walk forward, the pet parents because Twinkles could have swallowed their babies in one gulp, and the trainer because the Chihuahuas were nervous-peeing all over the place. Yeah, it wasn't a good scene. When I had packed up to go home that first night, the teacher handed me an envelope with a cash refund plus a twenty-dollar bonus and an "I'd very much like it if you don't come back." Poor Twinkles. It wasn't his fault he was so big, and yet still thought of himself as puppy-sized.

I unlocked the door, and Twinkles immediately headed

to his favorite napping spot in a stream of sunlight. I sat down at the table across from Kay and pulled the white paper bag with the beginnings of an oil stain closer. I closed my eyes and opened the bag, leaning in to inhale the scent of Heaven - a Philly cheesesteak from Sicily Sandwiches. I just knew that when I passed through the Pearly Gates, St. Peter would be handing me a bag just like this one. Breathing in the scent of melted cheese and french-fry grease was a religious experience. "Thank you for this food, amen," I said, and crossed myself before I opened my eyes and ripped the bag open to use as a placemat. "What are you eating?"

"A salad." Kay opened a Styrofoam container. "I filled my daily fat and sugar quotient with the box of doughnuts Cheatham brought in this morning." She jabbed her fork into the mound of greens and wrinkled her nose. "Penance," she said, then took a bite.

I looked up as another group of people waddled past Hooch's window. I could see them heading to Nicky's. It seemed the restaurant business was doing fine. I wondered what had happened to make things fall off here at the bar.

"Nicky's is doing good." Kay was always good at reading my mind. "Maybe we should have eaten over there to see if we could figure out the demographic."

"Cyborgs," I said.

"Come again?" Kay shoved a tomato into her mouth.

"They'd have to have iron stomachs. I don't need to head over there ever again. I did that once. I ordered a Calzone alla Nicky that really should have been called Crap alla Nicky, or maybe it would be Crud alla Nicky. Joe was telling me the other day that Nicky's dishwasher told him that Nicky's lunch specialty was whatever was left over from the night before and nuked in the microwave." I shrugged. "Dishwasher grapevine." I spread a bar towel on my lap, and because I knew what would happen when the juices in my cheesesteak started to run, I tucked another in the top of my stretchy t-shirt. "I prefer my lunch without stomach cramps, thank you very much." I took a huge bite and chewed it slowly, moaning a little under my breath.

Kay chuckled.

I shoved the bag a little closer to her. I knew she'd start sneaking fries any second, since she was on her fourth bite of penance. I might as well make it a little easier for her.

Sure enough, she reached out to grab one. "You know," she pointed the fry at me, "we could have just sat at the bus stop in front of the police station and watched all the cop cars go by. You could have ranked them for me on talent, agility and speed."

"The cars or the men?" I winked, then slurped up some lime-aid.

"Speaking of men, how did things go with Dick last night?" Kay asked.

"To be honest, watching him work, I was getting a little warm and tingly. He's a really talented man. Smart. Nice. I like him a lot."

"But?"

"He's out of uniform and into a suit. If I enjoyed the company of law enforcement in suits, that would mean there would be no cutoff date. Even good coupons expire."

Kay picked up the other half of my sandwich and bit off a good-sized chunk. "You're comparing Dick to coupons?" she asked from behind a hand she used to cover her still-full mouth.

"Yup. There are terms and limitations. For me, it's men in blue uniforms with a full tool belt buckled around their hips."

"And a shiny badge."

"That goes without saying."

After we finished with our lunches, I pushed back from the table. "Are you busy with your work stuff or can you help me get Daphne spiffed up? I want her all ready for tonight's crowd."

"You hope there's a crowd." Kay gathered the garbage and went to chuck it in the trash.

"I do indeed." I grabbed Daphne around the waist and hauled her upright. Twinkles lifted his head to look at me, decided I wasn't doing anything exciting, and flumped his head back on the ground with a wide-mouthed yawn.

Kay sidled around the back of the bar to get the clothes bag. "You really want to make her the mascot?"

"Think of it this way. Every successful bar or brand has some sort of gimmick. Ours is—well, was, maybe it still is— Badge Bunny Booze. Now, not everyone outside of this community even knows what a badge bunny is. So, tonight we can debut Daphne with the booze. And I got her a little addition to her outfit."

"Pray tell."

I smiled and pulled my handbag over to pull out a very fine pair of bunny ears that I'd picked up at the costume shop.

"Cute! I love them. And look, you found ears the same color as her hair." Kay snatched them from my hand and held them up to Daphne. She nodded her head left, then right. "Well, the bar will be dim. It'll work. Very nice. So I'm looking at poor Daphne, and I'm thinking she looks less like a friend of the Easter Bunny and more like an elf for Santa Claus who slid down a few chimneys. What did Dick say about the dust?"

"I can wash it off. Warm soap and water. He took a

bunch of photos. Made a bunch of cards. He's also going to attach all of that to Peter's report. There's nothing about the mannequin that he said needed to be preserved." I looked out the window as a cop car drove by. "You know, I should call Peter."

"Preserved?"

"He said that all of the evidence was gathered and the mannequin didn't need to be preserved for any reason. I needed to make sure that was the case because if Daphne's going to hang out in the bar, she's not going to be a good source of evidence any more. She'll just be a mannequin."

"Did Dick think there was a crime?"

"Only that some poor guy abused himself in public. They might be able to make a case for littering. But no. Dick was just trying to get on my good side again. Though he never was on my bad side. He even asked me out for a steak dinner and a movie."

"That was mighty big of him."

"That wasn't the part of him that was mighty big, poor guy." I winked. I headed back to get one of Joe's bins and some soap and hot water.

━━━

It was odd washing Daphne. Creepy-odd. It was like playing nurse and bathing someone who was paralyzed. Well, more like petrified. Her glass eyes seemed to follow my every move. I tried not to look her in the face. I found myself being extra gentle in the tickly places. It took some effort to get all of the dusting powder off.

Kay lifted Daphne up while I inched a pair of cotton briefs up her legs. They were from the drawer of panties I wore when I was on my period and felt crabby and crampy and just wanted to be comfortable. I thought Daphne would be down with that. Next, I got her sundress on, and Kay combed out Daphne's hair while I strapped on the sandals.

"She's really cute," Kay said. "This dress really flatters her."

We set her on the bar stool at the L of the bar where she was semi-protected from getting knocked over. I worked to adjust her so she was in a natural pose. I knew many a guy who would be drooling to take out a girl like this. As a matter of fact... I pulled out my phone and took a quick picture. Then forwarded it with the text.

I've found your next girlfriend, Kay-approved!

As I put my phone back in my pocket, I turned to see Kay considering Daphne. "You know, if she was animated, this is the kind of girl Mr. Happy would go for," she said.

Great minds!

Mr. Happy is the pet name Kay called her sometimes-boyfriend. It's actually the name he gave his penis. And it's absurd. And that's why she calls him that to me behind his back. His real name is Terrance Pattenson. Yes, *the* Terrance Pattenson, Internet phenom with his threemillion clicks-a-day following.

Terrance and Kay have an on-again/off-again relation-ship that was currently flipped to the 'off' position. It was just a matter of time until she turned him on again. And to be honest, I hoped they'd get back together soon. Kay always smiled more when they were together. Maybe the text I just sent him would get a conversation going. It rarely took much more than a little push to get their motors to turn over–I just couldn't figure out why they kept stalling out.

I looked from Kay to Daphne. They actually looked really similar. They both had long, silky red hair, though

Kay was more strawberry blond and Daphne had a lot more auburn. They were both about five-foot four and slender. They both had a winsome look to their faces, with a slight scoop in their noses, a smattering of girl-next-door freckles and intelligent eyes. Did I just think that Daphne had intelligent eyes? They're glass, for Pete's sake. *I need to call Peter,* I thought parenthetically. Glass or not, Daphne's and Kay's eyes were the same shade of blue green. "You two could be sisters," I said, looking down at my phone screen as it buzzed to let me know I had an incoming text.

Is Kay there with you? Terrence wrote.

"Looks like you have a message from Mr. Happy on my phone."

Kay snatched my phone from me to read. "Did you just text him?"

Some people liked relationships, and thrived in them. I was not one of those people. Connor said I'd come around when I was more mature, then he pulled my ponytail and kissed my nose. That was last week, so I wouldn't hold my breath on me changing anytime soon. But my feelings about not searching for my own deep, meaningful romance, didn't extend to other people. As a matter of fact, I enjoyed relationships as a spectator sport. There was something about watching the tango, like a bad rom-com. But for Kay, well, I just wanted her to be happy, and cutting off Terrence from her life hadn't done that.

"Terrance has got his thumb on the Internet pulse. I thought he might have an idea about what I should do with Daphne," I said. "I really need this bar thing to work out because I *hate* pantyhose."

"What?" She said looking up and catching my eye. "Pantyhose?"

"You like him. You miss him. And this is like a win-win scenario."

She pulled her brow into a tight scowl.

"He gets the opportunity to prove his prowess by coming up with an idea. You get to be swept off your feet by his amazing abilities. You get laid, and I just might get a happy ending." I stared at the floor for a second. "That didn't come out right." I shook my head. "You know what I mean. This could work out really well for all of us."

"Terrance may not be on the market."

"Kay, get real, he was back in touch like twenty seconds after I texted him and was asking about you. Who does that unless they're interested?"

She looked down at the text, looked up at the ceiling, looked back to the text, and started tapping away on my phone. Before I could ask another question, the door swung open and in walked Hooch's nemesis, Nicky,, with his son Georgi in tow.

CHAPTER 7

Nicky sauntered in like he owned the place. His gray hair was slicked back, and a bowling shirt with the restaurant's logo—an N circled with Caesar's olive leaf victory wreath—draped over his soup-chicken of a body. "Where's Hooch?" he asked.

I moved to stand protectively in front of Daphne; I didn't know why. And Twinkles, with a rumbling growl, came to stand protectively in front of me.

Nicky strode up to the bar and slid onto a stool, a wary eye on Twinkles. He smelled strongly of espresso and garlic, a combination that made the cheesesteak in my stomach roll over. I felt a little green around the gills.

"Your dishwasher told my dishwasher—well, you know how rumors get spread—that Hooch ran for the hills and left you in charge."

"Since Joe speaks Hungarian and your dishwasher speaks Italian, there might have been a glitch in the translation. Let me clarify for you. Hooch is taking a well-deserved vacation. And I, as the manager of the bar, will carry on while he enjoys his walks on a breathtaking beach, the swell of the sea, and surely a beautiful woman or two on his arm."

"If that's the tune you want to play, then fine," Nicky said. "My understanding was that you signed partnership papers with him. And I wanted you to know that I'm in a position to offer you a generous amount to buy the building. Enough that maybe you could find your own beach to walk on and enjoy the surf and sun."

"No thanks."

"I think you should at least—"

"Not interested." I said it as nicely as I could. I mean, I'd hate for my dad to get word that I wasn't being as respectful as I should be to an elderly man. But inwardly, I cringed. I knew that he talked smack about me behind my back. He was one of those men who thought Italian men, with their hot Latin libidos, were the studs of the world, but *women* should be pristine vessels. If all their women were Madonnas, I had no clue whom he thought these Italian stallions were romping in the clover with. But I knew he slut-shamed me for the exact same behaviors he held in high esteem for guys, a double standard I found pathetic and medieval.

I looked over at Nicky's son Georgi. I'd met him a few times when he was bouncing a ball in the alleyway waiting for his dad to finish up. Georgi was a sweet guy. Shy. He had warm, brown, puppy-like eyes that were endearing. He probably had the intellectual capacity of an eight-year-old, though I'd guess he was in his early thirties. Where he got his tall genes, I'm not sure. He stood about six-two while his dad was more my height.

"I don't think I ever introduced you to my boy," Nicky said, gesturing to where Georgi stood by the door. "Georgi, here. He's a great catch." He nodded his head. "He likes blondes. You're the kind of woman he'd date. He's going to make some lucky woman one hell of a husband." He looked me dead in the eye. "Maybe that lucky girl could be you, huh?" He waved Georgi over. "This is Roberta," he introduced me.

"She likes to be called BJ," Georgi said with a little smile. He lifted his hand about three inches and gave me a wave.

"Roberta," Nicky said sternly. "BJ isn't ladylike. She shouldn't let the boys call her that."

Georgi looked confused. He turned from his father to me with his brow pulled together. I thought I'd clear it up for him. "My friends call me BJ. And we're friends, Georgi."

Georgi turned back to his father. "BJ is my friend. She plays ball with me in the alley, and she lets me hold Twinkles's lead when she's taking him for a walk."

Twinkles heard his name and the little stump of his tail waggled over the floor. He stuck his neck out so Georgi could pet him behind the ears—an honor Twinkles didn't afford everyone. It told me everything I needed to know about Georgi.

Nicki seemed to mull the situation over for a hot second, and then he went right back to trying to sell Georgi. "He's going to be a good man. He has great potential. You should come and have dinner at my restaurant. You can share a plate of spaghetti—a plate of spaghetti for two. You like spaghetti? I like spaghetti. Georgi wants to buy your bar."

Spaghetti alla Nicky was the cheapest thing on the menu, and I noticed he said we could share a plate. I looked over at Georgi, who had plopped down on the floor and was sitting cross-legged. Twinkles's head rested on Georgi's thigh while he got his ears rubbed. What Georgi probably wanted was a hot fudge sundae and a game of catch. "I'm not selling the bar. Period. End of discussion."

"Listen to an old man who has nothing to gain from the situation other than to help you out. Set you on a better course. Sell the bar—it's not a nice job for a good girl. Get married. Have kids. A woman is happiest in her own kitchen."

"Barefoot and pregnant?"

"Exactly! Look, this ship is going down. When a ship is about to go down, all the rats jump ship. You know why? They want to survive."

"I'm not a rat. And do you know what happens to the rats that jump off? They're out in the middle of the ocean with no way to survive and they drown. That's not a great analogy if you're trying to get me to bail."

The door swung open, rescuing me from having to continue. Kay ran over to welcome Terrance. "Excuse me, someone I'm scheduled to meet has arrived. It was great catching up with you, Nicky...Georgi." I gave Georgi a smile. "If you have your ball, I'll be glad to play catch later."

"Cool," he said, scrambling up after planting a kiss on Twinkles's head, then headed out the door. His father shifted off the stool and followed him out, leaving a wake of disgust as he went. I'd need to fumigate. I moved to the back of the bar to grab a can of Lysol.

Just as the door was about to swing shut, Nicky stuck his head back around the crack. "With that whole ship analogy that you aren't happy with, you should know the storm is rising. There's nothing you can do to stop it." The door slammed and Kay rolled her eyes so far up into her head she could see gray matter.

"What the hell was that? Sounded like he was threatening you," Terrance said.

"Meh," I said, and headed over to give Terrance a hug. "This is a wonderful and perfectly timed surprise. You must have been in the neighborhood to show up so quickly."

He took the seat recently vacated by Nicky while I sprayed the disinfectant.

"I was up the block at Kay's office. I'd dropped in to say hi to her, see if she didn't want to grab a bite to eat, but she wasn't there. And boom, I get your text." Terrance turned to study the mannequin. "That's just freaky."

"Her name is Daphne," Kay said.

I moved over to set the Lysol on the bar, then sat down next to Terrance. "I was hoping to use her as a draw somehow. What I was really hoping was that you might have an idea or two how I could do that."

"She should make social media go nuts!" Terrance leaned forward to look closer at Daphne. "She's so lifelike, it's crazy." He reached out and flicked Daphne on the cheek, just like I had. Reassured this wasn't some kind of complex joke, he sat back and contemplated her. "I think we can spin it," he said after a long minute. "The Mannequin Challenge is all the rage now. Maybe you can do a short video and post it on social media, something like, 'Can you spot the mannequin?' Throw Hooch's name in and the street..."

"Do you think that something so simple would draw a crowd?" Kay asked.

"It drew me here," he said. He stared at Kay and their eyes held. Kay's cheeks flushed, and I saw how much that affected Terrance. They belonged together. They loved each other. But somehow, they could never get the puzzle pieces to fit properly.

"Well, I'm sure you were beckoned by the warm-blooded woman here, not this thing," I said. "But while you're here, it would be great if you could help me figure a way to get Daphne to solve my financial woes."

"Yeah, Hooch's is now Bobbi Jax's," Kay said. "She needs the best, and most affordable way to get bodies in these seats."

"Congrats BJ. I think we should toast to your new role and to your future success," he said drumming his hands on the bar. "Do you still have that Badge Bunny Booze?"

"Coming right up," I scooted around and poured him a tumbler.

He took a thoughtful sip, then said, "This scotch is so smooth." He smacked his lips. "And there's a subtle undertone. What is that?"

Kay and I looked at each other and grinned. "Cherries and thyme," Kay said.

"I can tell there's a story behind that recipe." He wiggled his brow. "I bet it's a good one too."

I laughed. "Yeah, but I swore an oath never to reveal the origins."

Terrance lifted his glass to Daphne. "*Sláinte,*" he said, wishing her good health in Irish. "Okay, having Daphne here is a good start, but you need to play it up more. Make it a contest and have a winner get a date with the mannequin..."

I tipped my head. I wasn't sure I trusted Daphne going on a date with a stranger.

"I'm just throwing out ideas," he said.

I nodded and sat quietly, letting his creative mind churn.

"Nope," he said. "Maybe?" He put his hands over his eyes then opened them like a peek-a-boo reveal. "Don't be lonely tonight. Or, here." He handed Kay his phone. "Snap a picture with me and what did you call her?"

"Daphne," Kay said taking the phone and framing the picture.

"Yeah, Daphne. I'll put it online with the tag, 'Come on down and meet the bunny behind those Badge Bunny blues?'"

"For that you get another one on the house." I poured another finger of scotch into his empty glass. "But Kay has to drive you home and tuck you into bed to make sure you get there safely."

"I'm down with that." Terrance grinned as he lifted the tumbler to his lips.

Kay was giving me a stink face. What can I say? I was a friend looking out for her best interests.

The door opened and I expected it to be Nicky again. In walked a deputy sheriff in a brown uniform, wearing his campaign hat. The large brim hid part of his handsome face, but the uniform was a put-off. I liked my guys in blue. His badge still gleamed, but it didn't do anything for me. Brown was a downer color. As he walked toward us, I thought that calling Peter was getting higher and higher on my list of things to do.

"Is James Bradly in?" the deputy asked.

"Sorry, but he's on vacation. I'm the manager left in charge, though."

"And your name?"

"Roberta Reid."

His eye caught on Daphne. He moved over and stared at her. I could see the cogs whirling.

I watched him closely.

He reached out and flicked her cheek.

I could tell that something about this mannequin was pulling at him, and he was rumbling around in his brain trying to figure out what.

He lifted his finger and wagged it at her, then turned his head a bit and looked out of the corner of his eye, then shook his head.

"Does she look familiar?" I asked, half-hoping he had an explanation. The other half was hoping he didn't and wouldn't take her away. Good angel. Bad angel.

"She does. If she were human, I'd swear I've seen her before, I just can't remember where. That's a little freaky."

He held out an envelope and I reflexively took it.

He tipped his hat. "You've been served. Thank you, ma'am." He moved back out the door with a deputized swagger, and I pouted reading the words in large print: CITATION.

"What the hell is this about?" I asked, as the door swung shut behind him.

Kay came over and took it from my hands, and read it over.

"Well, this didn't take long. Seems as if Hooch's is now under investigation. The ABC— Alcohol Beverage Control —is going to want to see your accounting books, Bobbi Jax. Sounds like you'll be getting some unscheduled law enforcement visits as well."

I pushed my hair out of my face and frowned. "That might be nice. I did want to make this place a refuge for the boys in blue." My remark fell flat. There was nothing positive about this turn of events.

"Yeah, but if they find something, you're looking at fines, misdemeanor charges, and possibly losing the bar completely."

"What are they accusing me of?" I moved over and positioned myself cheek to cheek with Kay so I could read over her shoulder.

"Here: they say that you've been serving underage

drinkers." She ran her finger under the words she was deciphering out of legal-ese for me. "And serving alcohol that isn't labeled."

"That's preposterous." I scrunched my brows together. "Do you think Nicky's behind this?" I asked. "Everyone who's been hanging out at the bar lately has been as old as my grandpa. I actually need to attract a younger crowd, the newbies just out of the academy so I can start them on a life-long loyalty kick with Hooch's."

"We need to get this bar pumping this weekend, then," Terrance said.

"Agreed. Because if they come after me in earnest, I'm going to need money to either pay a fine or potentially to bail me out of a cell." I could feel the stress tightening my muscles. I needed some relief that would come in a Peter package. Or to phrase it more precisely, Peter's package. "I'm going to let you two catch up. I have to make a call."

I pulled Peter's contact up: **Are you on duty? I'm wondering if you wanted to pick up where we left off,** I texted.

Peter: **YOU left off. You dropped me like I was hot.**

BJ: **You ARE hot ;) and I've been thinking about you. HARD.**

Peter: **I'm on duty in an hour. Where are you?**

BJ: **In the back room at the bar, feeling lonely and deprived.**

Peter: **I can be there in five minutes.**

BJ: **Are you dressed for work? Is your tool belt in place?**

Peter: **I was just sitting here wishing I had a good place to put my tool.**

BJ: **Maybe I could help you out :D**

Peter: **Give me ten and I'll be ready for you, my badge all shined up.**

BJ: **Make it seven and I'll shine your badge for you ;)**

CHAPTER 8

I YAWNED and stretched and checked the clock. Noon. No wonder Twinkles was whining by the door with his legs crossed. I swung my covers off and planted my feet on the floor. Going to bed at four a.m. didn't work great with my biorhythms. Just sayin'.

Last night a rowdy bunch of college boys came in around one. They made a mess and left at closing. I wasn't complaining. They had a mighty big bar tab that was a pleasure to ring up. But Joe was hacking up a lung, and I didn't have enough alcohol in the bar to kill whatever virus was taking over his sinus cavities. I sent him home as soon as I locked the doors at two.

Usually after the bar closed at two, Hooch told me to go right home. I was going to have to get used to later hours now that Hooch was gone. He and Joe had been the ones who finished up if there was anything left to do since Hooch didn't like me out until the wee hours of the morning. I didn't like to be out until the wee hours of the morning either - even if I had Twinkles with me.

Two-thirty to ten-thirty worked out great for me and my

beauty sleep. Four a.m. to noon, though, and I looked like a horror show. Bags under my eyes, frighteningly pale skin, and hair from hell. I didn't deserve this, I thought as I examined myself in the mirror. I looked like I'd just woken up from a bender, and I hadn't had a single sip of booze. Funny how alcohol becomes a turn-off after you've cleaned up someone's emptied stomach enough times after they missed the john.

John...I haven't called him in a while. I wonder what he's up to. What I really wondered was if he was still dating Amy-what's-her-name or if he might have been single again...

I puffed out some air and forced myself to stand. My muscles ached. My bones groaned. This was ridiculous. I'd just turned twenty-two. You'd have thought I was ready for a nursing home the way my body was complaining.

Yeah, four o'clock was going to take some getting used to. At least I had Twinkles to keep me safe. I looked over at where he laid by the door with his tongue lolling out, dripping dog slobber on the floor.

Twinkles as a guard dog was a little bit of Russian roulette with my safety. I thought that he was probably more into the atmospherics of a threat than being an actual threat. Twinkles worked that angle to the max. He'd lift his lips to show just a peek of his ferocious, white, canine canines and let menace rumble around his gonads where it picked up a shot of testosterone which he then slid up his throat, over his vocal chords, and rumbled out in a growl that usually caused the person he focused on a good dose of fear paralysis and maybe a couple drops of pee.

Speaking of pee... I shuffled toward the bathroom. "Me first. I'll take you in a second," I told Twinkles when he bounced his nose on the strand of bells tied to my front door handle, his alert that he needed to go.

I slogged through the bathroom door, not bothering to close it behind me. I've never actually seen Twinkles leap into action. I'm not sure he would. But he can threaten like a big dog. Hmm, that's kind of redundant, since he is a *big* dog, I thought, dragging the shower curtain to the side and starting the water. How about - he could growl like a war dog who'd like nothing better than chomping down on the enemy. Better? Good enough.

My thoughts would probably get more coherent after some coffee. Twinkles rang the bells a little more insistently. "Five minutes," I called to him, then pulled my nightshirt over my head and checked to see if the hot water had kicked in.

When I opened the lid on my clothes hamper to deposit my shirt, something was dinging inside. I fumbled through my dirty clothes until I pulled out the jeans I'd been wearing last night. I fished out my phone, still stuck in the pocket. I'd missed several messages, including from Terrance, Kay, and a number I didn't recognize. Kay had freaking left me a voicemail. Huh, that was weird. Concern brushed over me as I called my voice mailbox but abated as soon as I heard the excitement in her recording.

"I know you're still sleeping," Kay began, "but it looks like Terrence pulled off a miracle! That post is lighting up social media. Call me."

Connor had left a voice message, too. But he was on duty and that's his modus operandi when he was driving his cop car. "Kay told me you might need my help tonight since your gimmick is gaining traction from Terrance's video. Anyway, I'll be there around five when you open." I imag-ined Connor for a moment in his crisp blue uniform, sauntering...I shook my head to clear the image. Connor fantasies were a sure ticket to discomfort, and I'd never let anything happen between us. Neither would he. Our relationship was much too special.

I turned my attention, instead, to a text from Terrance: **Told you it would light up the web like fire. Already 200,000 views on the video, and a 138,000 likes and tons of shares. I know you're wondering about the video. Kay and I filmed a little bit while you were visiting with Peter. I sent a file to your cloud. This is so hot. See you tonight so we can start the badge bunny fun!**

I had never known Terrance to write such a long text. Usually his texts were: **Wazup?** Or **Gotcha**. Or even **Tonight at eight**. But more than three or four words? Shocking.

Film? Cloud? Too early. Okay, it was after noon, but still... too early. I put the phone on the sink and climbed into the shower to try to become a human again. I hurried myself along when Twinkles scratched at the door and made a pitiful whimpering noise.

I jumped out of the shower, toweled off, pulled on some yoga pants and a sports shirt with a built-in bras, then slipped my feet into a pair of flip-flops, grabbed my keys along with Twinkles' lead, and opened the door.

Twinkles barreled out the door, down the stairs where Mrs. Crabgrass was coming in with her groceries. He nosed past her and ran over to the three blades of grass that valiantly tried to survive urban life under the stop sign. I found him there, eyes rolled back in his head, obviously enjoying the pleasure of his relief. When he was done, he trotted over to me so I could clip his leash on and take him to the dog park.

I stopped by the corner café for a cup of coffee. Black. High-test. Tall. Hopefully, reviving. I sat on the bench and let Twinkles go and sniff his friends' butts, cause that's what dog friends do. Like I always say, to each his own. Just as long as it was consensual.

I took as big a gulp of the scalding hot coffee as my pain sensors would allow, then opened my cloud. There was a video of Terrance with his arm draped around Daphne.

"You think you can beat Daphne here at the mannequin challenge? Look at her." Terrance started making faces at Daphne. Daphne didn't move. "Look at her!" He started snapping his fingers right in front of her eyes. "No blinking. Can you believe it? Can you do that?" He turned his charismatic smile toward the camera and pointed. "I challenge you! Come out to Hooch's and test your skills. The best mannequin wins a running bar tab for a whole night!"

Kay could be heard clearing her throat off camera.

"No?" Terrance shook his head looking like a kid who just had his lollipop taken away. "Yeah you're right. That would be illegal. Well, we'll hook you up with something equally cool." Grin. Wink. God, he's a total schmoozer. I could see why he got Kay's panties in a bunch. Luckily, he wasn't a boy in blue, so there was no problem with me being able to overlook his sex appeal.

He made some weird hand sign and ended on "Let's get this party on fleek."

I rolled my eyes at that bit. *Fleek.* What the heck was fleek? I typed the address for the Urban Dictionary into my phone to look up a definition. God, I felt old. I sniffed and took another hit of caffeine. Twenty-two and I couldn't keep up.

⸻

"You know I can't take you tonight," I told Twinkles. I was putting on my earrings and giving my hair one last fluff. I could see him through my open bedroom door, sitting in the foyer with his lead in his mouth, ready for action. He looked at me and cocked his head to the right. A short whine, then he put his lead down and gave a bark of disagreement.

"Well, where are you going to stay?" I asked, checking my phone.

Kay: **Heading to the bar**

I walked down the hall toward Twinkles and shoved my cell phone into my back pocket. "In the back office? *All* night?" I raised my brows. "You know you hate sitting back there all by yourself."

Again, he barked, then picked up his lead and moved to block the front door.

"I don't know," I said as I bent down to pet him and pat his sides. He leaned into me, waggling his little stub tail. Just like he knew he would, the little conniver, he made my will melt into a puddle of 'who's-a-good-boy?' feelings. I reached for his lead and clipped it in place. "Alright, but no chewing on the furniture—" Before I could finish, Twinkles raced down the stairs and right passed Mrs. Crabgrass, out to my car, where he waited patiently to be chauffeured.

⸻

At Hooch's, I walked in practically shaking with excitement. Joe was coughing in the back. That wasn't okay. He needed to go to bed and get better. I reached for the Lysol to give myself a cloud of disinfectant to walk through as I went to send him home. You know, some people just embrace their true spirit, and Joe was one of those people. He loved to wash dishes. *Loved* it. Personally, I couldn't understand. And my non-comprehension had nothing to do with Joe's very loose grasp of the English language. His serene smile didn't need translation – but Lord have mercy, he needed another way to meditate until whatever alien creature was living in his nose got euthanized.

I sprayed a cloud and took two steps, sprayed another and took two more. I arrived in the service area and said, "Bye-bye." I waved and pointed at the door.

He pointed at the steins that were already perfectly clean.

"No." I shook my head. "Please go home and take care of yourself." I pointed again at the door.

Joe arched backward and gave a whole-body sneeze. I ducked and covered my head with my arm as I sprayed the air above me with the disinfectant, hoping the droplets that were landing on my head and bare skin was the Lysol. *Please, God, let it be the Lysol.*

With the saddest face I've ever seen on him, and drooping shoulders of defeat, Joe hung up his apron and with a sigh, moved out the door.

"Feel better!" I called. "I'll see you soon."

I emptied the Lysol can into the air. Shit, I had no dish-washer tonight.

Someone knocked and I went to open the door for Connor and Kay… and looky here, the Ice Queen had come along for the ride. Twinkles looked her in the eye and growled. I bent over to grab his collar—as if I could stop Twinkles if he took a lunge. He outweighed me, and I didn't really care if he tackled Ashley or not. "Twinkles, if she offers you any Turkish Delights, don't eat them," I whispered. That was a little piece of advice I picked up from Edmund when I read *The Lion, the Witch, and the Wardrobe* in my high school English Lit class. I had counseled Connor the same way back then. But sadly, he didn't follow my advice. He'd let Ashley slip him some candy, and now he was under her evil spell. I wholeheartedly believed that was true, because Connor deserved so much better than Ashley and her damned resting bitch face. Boy, would I love to smack some of the nasty right off her. She'd probably feel better for it, too.

Kay probably picked up my thoughts in the ether. She caught my eye and shook her head. For Connor's sake, I bit my tongue and moved back to let them in. Connor barely got inside when Twinkles shook my hand off his neck and headbutted Connor's hip until Connor sat on the floor with his back to the side of the booth. Twinkles climbed into Connor's lap like he was a tiny puppy and rested his jowls over Connor's shoulder. Connor rubbed Twinkles's back like he was a toddler being put down for a nap. And Twinkles was clearly in Heaven.

Ashley had moved over to Daphne. "I came down to see this thing after catching the video online. She really does look so real." Ashley reached out to touch Daphne's cheek. She looked back at me. "Okay that's all," she said. She headed toward Connor but when she got within arm's length, her presence roused Twinkles from lullaby land. He growled at her approach, turning his head to bare his teeth and most of his gums. It stopped her mid-step.

Good boy. You get a juicy bone for that.

"Love-muffins," she crooned from the middle of the room. "I know you'll be here for a few hours, but don't forget, we're to meet Daddy at the golf club tomorrow. Early to bed, early to rise." She kissed her hand, then waved it at each of us. I threw up a little in my mouth.

This girl had a way of rubbing her wealth in people's faces. It wasn't actually her money – it had trickled down the Randolph DNA chain and pooled in her parent's bank account. Her parents' money and connections had landed her a job at a big financial firm downtown. She was an up and comer. Just like my lunch.

CHAPTER 9

IT DIDN'T TAKE LONG from the neon sign to start flashing OPEN for the bar to fill up. Terrance was there playing King of the Internet, whooping it up and getting people involved in various drinking games he'd come up with. The one that was keeping me the busiest was the staring contest, where whoever laughed first took a shot. The more they drank, the shorter the time between pours.

Connor was in charge of the key basket. As people were getting toward the questionable zone, they'd get a free snack of their choice put in front of them in exchange for their name, phone number, address, and car keys. I'd be hailing Lyfts later to take them home. Or they'd show up sheepishly tomorrow to retrieve their keys. If they didn't hand over their keys, they got stamped with a day-glow dot on their hand and were cut off for the rest of the night. If someone started buying drinks for them, they were both escorted out. "Them's the rules, folks." I was not sending anyone out in the streets and putting others in danger to make a buck. But most people understood, and it was a good time. Busy. But good.

Music pumped, booze flowed, and there was barely standing room inside with the crowd spilling out into the garden area Hooch had never gotten a chance to use. Thank god for the cheap garden umbrella and dollar-store tea lights to illuminate the place. Combine that with some tiki torches against the mosquitos and, voila, atmosphere.

From the dress and style of those who showed up, we'd pulled in revelers from the happy hour places farther downtown in the business district, as well as the college kids, and some of the hipsters, too. Not too many had the swagger of a man who wore a blue uniform, but that was okay, too. Tonight was about making that cash register sing, and I was *liking* her tune.

Around ten-fifteen, the door opened again, and it was Channel 13's news crew. I rushed forward to greet them.

"Are you the manager?" Chloe Adams, the news anchor, asked. She stuck out her hand for a shake.

"Yes, welcome. Can I buy you and your crew a drink?"

"No, thank you. We need to fill some air tonight at eleven. We thought we'd come down and meet Daphne."

I extended my hand, and we moved toward the bar.

———

In and out, the news crew was efficient.

Kay came to my side. "How'd it go?"

"To tell the truth, I have no idea what they asked or what I said, I was so nervous. But I did point at Daphne and talk about how she was wonderful. I sounded drunk for sure."

"Well, maybe they'll have time to do some editing."

I glanced around at my patrons. "We look like a college

bar. There is no way we're going to draw in the right clientele from this."

"And by right, I'm assuming you mean cops? Bobbi Jax, you worry too much. This place is packed." She dragged a soothing hand down my arm. "You look beat. Maybe you should take five, have a drink and watch the crowd some."

I took Kay's advice and poured myself a cola with a splash of lime. I leaned against the prep counter and surveyed the crowd. I liked the laughter. I liked the noise. What I didn't particularly like was that Ashley kept texting Connor. I could tell it was her because he made the B.O. face every time he looked down at his phone. Finally, he turned it off and shoved it in his back pocket.

As Connor blended into the crowd, another guy caught my attention. Unlike the others who were dressed for a casual evening, this guy was dressed for an important date. I looked around to see what the object of his affections looked like. And his gaze was glued to Daphne.

He shouldered his way over to her. Approached with a shy smile. He reached out and caught at a fold in her skirt, rubbed the fabric between his fingers, and closed his eyes. The woman sitting on the stool next to Daphne gave the guy a look, gathered her things and abandoned her seat. The man in his dark grey suit and his lovely cobalt blue tie slid onto the stool. His hand slipped possessively to Daphne's hip. He sent her a moony stare with warm affectionate eyes.

I looked over at Connor and didn't blink while I sent death rays to the back of his head. It never took long. He felt me zapping him and turned, offering up a smile. I waved him over. As he moved around the end of the bar, I turned to cut some lemons. Really, I was watching the suited guy in the bar mirror. I indicated the guy with my chin as Connor came up beside me, leaning in until we were shoulder to shoulder. Connor smelled good, fresh, like laundry soap.

"Have you seen Kay giving that guy drinks?" I asked.

"He came in just a couple minutes ago." Connor shifted. "Is he holding hands with Daphne?"

I turned and took an order from Kay, then reached for beer steins. "Yup. Weird, huh?"

"Let's keep an awareness."

Connor talked that way – "keep an awareness." Yeah, it does good things for me. Sigh. Too bad I loved him, which made him a no-go. That and his relationship with the Ice Queen meant I was safe from making a fool of myself. The perv on the stool next to Daphne, on the other hand, didn't seem to mind making a fool of himself. He was now deep in earnest conversation with her.

I passed the tray of beers to Kay and watched as the guy moved his hand to the small of Daphne's back possessively, protectively as people moved by.

"Rum and coke and a scotch rocks, please," someone ordered.

I filled the glasses mechanically. Could this perv be *the* perv who had taken Daphne to the azalea bushes? Hmmm.

Kay bumped her hip against mine. "Did you see the guy with the suit?"

"Fascinating individual," I said.

"Do you think that could be the guy from the park?" Kay asked.

That's why I like Kay – her mind goes where mine goes, no matter how twisted. I gave her a wink. "Nothing like the present to find out." I rounded to the back of the bar, filled my newest orders and sidled down to meet the guy. "Hey, can I get you something to drink?" I asked.

"Oh, uh, yes," he said, with a delicate flutter of his

fingers near the knot of his tie. "Could I have a Juliet and Romeo cocktail?"

"Juliet and Romeo," I said and drummed a coming-right-up tattoo on the bar. I pulled out my phone to look up the recipe. I'd never heard of such a concoction before. People liked to try to stump me. I'd had a lot of free time at the bar where I memorized different drinks and different ways to make them, but yeah, no one has ever asked for a Juliet and Romeo before. Really, I served four products. Beer on tap, beer in in a bottle, beer in a pitcher, and Badge Bunny Booze.

I put a drink in front of him. "Sorry, we don't have any cucumber. But this is close. Why don't you try it out? If you don't like it, we'll try something else."

"Oh, thank you." He wriggled around on the stool, then slid a look over to Daphne and gave her a wink as he lifted his glass, as if to toast her. He looked at me as he took a sip. A smile slid across his face. "Lovely. Yes." He took another sip then put it on the napkin.

I rested my elbows on the bar, laced my fingers, and planted my chin on my hands, settling in for a good chat while Kay filled drink orders. "I've never seen you in here before, have I? Do you work around here?"

"Oh no. No. This is my first time. Though I do work over in Clamber Industrial Park."

"Yeah?" I asked. "What do you do for a living?"

"I'm an engineer. A *plastics* engineer." Another glance at Daphne, a slight blush, and he dipped his head.

"You and our friend here seem to be getting along very nicely." I smiled and nodded. "Are you just now meeting? Or perhaps you knew her before she came to Hooch's?"

His face flushed an even deeper shade of red. "I saw her

on the Internet." He reached out and laid his hand on Daphne's knee. "She's such a pretty girl." He turned and smiled at Daphne, then turned back to me. "Could you tell me, please, what are you going to do with her? Is she going to stay here at the bar from now on?"

CHAPTER 10

LAST NIGHT HAD BEEN the best night! I sat in the back office tallying receipts with Twinkles burrowed under the desk, keeping my feet warm in his fur. I was feeling a little tipsy on the success as I worked. When my cellphone rang, I answered with a grin. "Hey ho!" I said, as Kay's name came up on the screen.

"I didn't expect to get you out of bed so early." Kay said. "Whatcha doin'?"

"Getting drunk on all the numbers I'm putting in my ledger from last night. Did you know we did more business in one night than we did all of last month?"

"I don't mean to be a downer, but that money is going to come in and go right on back out. I talked to Cheatham about your citation, and he says that if you end up needing to fight this, it could bleed you dry. So keep your nose especially clean."

"The only thing dirty about me are my thoughts. Speaking of dirty thoughts, I thought you'd be draped all over Terrance last night. I looked up, and you're flirting outrageously with someone with a bad boy vibe so strong it could melt a girl's panties."

"You saw him? Wasn't he yum?" Kay stalled and made a weird *rrrr* noise into the receiver with a wrinkled nose. "Do you think Terrance saw us together?"

"Was that an act? Were you trying to make Mr. Happy sad?"

"Me? No. I don't play games like that. I'd feel bad, though, if I was flirting with someone in front of Terrance. It seems wrong, even if we've broken up."

"Your breakups never last long." I rubbed my toes into Twinkles's coat, and he moaned and stretched with pleasure. "Besides, he'd left by then. I never did pass you his message. I got caught up. I'm sorry."

"That's okay."

"Terrance said he had to take the red eye to New York— he's on some show up there. But you're beautiful, he loves you, and he'll text you when he gets a free second."

"I'm beautiful? That doesn't sound like Terrance."

"Okay, he said you're a sex kitten that makes his motor hum. But I told him I'm not saying that."

Kay laughed.

"So, the new guy?"

"His name is Dante, if you can believe it. He said his mom read too many romance novels in her youth. His brothers fared worse. One of them is named Blade and the other is Ridge."

I rolled my eyes. "I don't believe it. He was pulling your leg."

"I wish he pulled my leg, and a few other body parts, too. That guy is woof! Really, really lovely."

"Terrance?" I reminded her.

"Is having fun. Why shouldn't I?"

"Because getting your body parts pulled by guys you aren't dating isn't really your thing." I tapped my fingers on my desk. I was feeling protective of Kay and Terrance's relationship. I didn't want some Dante guy walking in and spoiling things for them. "He *says* his name is Dante. Maybe that's his bar name. The one he uses when he's on the make."

"It didn't feel like he was on the make. He seemed very genuine. Very... interested in what I was saying. He didn't make any passes, and didn't say anything overtly flirtatious. But when I was talking to him, I felt like I was the most beautiful woman in the world. Like I was brilliant and scintillating and funny."

"Because you are."

"Pshh. I'm fine. But when I was talking to him I was *fine.* And that felt different. Tingly different." Kay bobbled her brow.

"Dante, though?"

"I'm not an idiot. I didn't believe him either, so he showed me his driver's license. Dante De Angelis."

"Holy smokes." I fanned my face. "That's over the top."

"Twenty-eight years old, six-foot two, a hundred and eighty pounds. He's an organ donor, and has brown eyes, though I'd call them melted dark chocolate."

"Yeah I bet you would. Is he a good kisser?"

"We haven't been on a date."

"Just checking on his powers of persuasion."

I heard a knock on the door and moved to answer it. Twinkles walked ahead of me. He growled at the man who stood at the front door. He was tall with almost black hair that hung in loose curls that brushed his shirt collar. Around six-foot two. Drop-my-panties hot and smiling at me through the glass. I held up a finger to ask him to wait. "Does Dante have a scar on his brow?"

"Yes, why?"

"I think he's here at the door. Why don't I stall him, and you can come down and flirt?"

"Yes, please!" Her face disappeared behind my phone's screensaver.

I dug the front door key out of the basket and went to let him in. Twinkles obviously didn't like that he'd been roused from his nap. He'd definitely gotten up on the wrong side of the floor. Hackles raised, he positioned himself between me and the guy, and wasn't budging. I had to lean forward to get the lock turned.

"Hi," he said. He started to extend his hand, but Twinkles rumbled deep in his chest.

"Excuse Twinkles, he just woke up from a nap. Can I help you?"

"Dante De Angelis," he said with lovely warm smile.

How Kay went home without bringing this guy in tow last night was beyond me. He wasn't even my type, and he had me on a slow simmer.

"I was here last night for your Daphne debut. You had quite the crowd." He smiled and reached for his wallet, flipping it open. "I'm a local artist." He pulled out his card and held it out, watching Twinkles cautiously. "I thought we might be able to support each other's business. Would it be okay if I came in for a quick moment?"

Twinkles rumbled again.

"Or perhaps we could make an appointment, if I caught you in the middle of something?"

"Yeah, sure, come on in. I just need to go in the back and get something for Twinkles to eat. He's looking at your leg like it might be tasty."

Dante shot me an understanding look tinged with a bit of concern for his personal safety.

"Come on, Twinkles," I said, gesturing Dante to a booth.

Twinkles followed me back out to the bar. "Can I get you a glass of water or something to drink?" I asked as I came into the main room.

"I'm fine, thank you. Big dog."

"Twinkles. He isn't feeling well. Sorry if he isn't on his best behavior today."

"Poor guy."

Twinkles went over to Dante and started sniffing him. When Dante stuck out his hand to pet Twinkles, Dante got another rumble that made him snatch his hand back. As well he should have. Poor Twinkles's upset stomach made him sound ferocious. I've never heard him make sounds like that before. I hoped the growl wouldn't turn into vomit. Me cleaning up dog puke in front of the romance-novel dude as Kay floated through the doors would put a damper on the birds-and-flowers ambiance Dante seemed to swirl around him. I poured myself a glass of cola and poured some water into a bowl in case Twinkles needed it.

Kay. Kay. Kay. I did believe she might have been in over her head with this one. This one was a stud-muffin on steroids. I contemplated Dante as I walked back across the open space to the booth. He had pushed over to the window, farther away from Twinkles. He had what looked like an artist's portfolio on the seat beside him. I wouldn't call this guy handsome, or even cute, but he was...something. Charismatic might be the right word.

Twinkles's muscles tightened as I got closer. I sat on the other side of the booth and Twinkles sat right beside me, alert. I was alert, too. I had a couple of bar rags with me ready to deploy at the first sign of dog spew.

Dante tapped his portfolio. "I'm an artist. I do mostly commercial properties, murals and the like. Oil paintings of the corporate presidents and CEOs."

"Can I see?"

He ran the zipper along the teeth, then flipped the leather cover off. I shuffled through the pages. They were really good. I was passing time waiting for Kay.

"I was here last night. You had a great crowd."

"It was a good night," I said, and turned to another group of work. These ones were of animals painted in a kaleidoscope of colors. They were astonishing. They were modern, yet he was able to capture the personalities of each animal. The horses were especially beautiful.

"I met one of your servers, Kay," he said, and though the lighting was dim, I thought he might be blushing a little bit. So this was his way to schmooze himself in to find out about Kay, huh?

"I expect her to be by here soon." I looked out the window. It would be just like her to arrive with amazingly serendipitous timing, sailing through the door at the mere taste of her name on Dante's lips. That thought made me grin.

Dante tipped his head and considered me. "Kay told me that you were running the bar and that you were trying to revive it. It's in a great space," Dante said. "Maybe a little close to the police department to make people feel comfortable – they might be concerned about getting pulled and checked all the time with so many cops around. Or on the other hand, maybe they feel safer because the cops are there. That might be a good pull for women."

"I hadn't considered either of those angles." I took a sip

of cola. "To be honest, the crowd that was here last night, while helpful, is not the crowd I'd like to encourage. I want this to be the go-to local cop bar."

Dante looked slowly around the bar space. The front was taken up by awning-protected windows. The back had a long L-shaped bar, where Daphne sat. A mirror and shelves took up the vertical space. The wall to the right was brick and had a little corridor that led to the bathrooms. His focus landed on the wall to the left. It was a plain white wall with a few tchotchkies hanging on it. Nothing exciting. Came off as drab, really. It was as if I was seeing the place through a new set of eyes as I followed Dante's gaze.

He sucked his upper lip between his teeth as he considered the wall. I imagined he was thinking of it as an empty canvas. "Do you have a theme here? Some way that you're marketing to cops?" he asked, turning back to me.

"We serve our house-brand Badge Bunny Booze. That's as close as we get to 'theme.'"

Dante looked over at Daphne. "Is that why your mascot is wearing ears? I thought a badge bunny was a girl who..." His gaze rested on me. "Sorry, you probably already know that since you run the place."

I met his gaze with pure innocence and blinked twice. "Probably know what?" I asked.

"That a badge bunny is a girl who likes to date cops."

I furrowed my brow. "Badge bunnies are girls that date cops?" I asked.

"Not date. They just..." He spun his head at the sound of the door opening.

There stood Kay, looking fresh and beautiful in a white sundress and gold sandals. Twinkles got up, went toward her, grabbed a mouthful of skirt and dragged Kay back to my side of the table.

I scooted over to give her space to join me. Kay bent to give me a kiss on the cheek and slid into the place I had been keeping warm for her.

"What's up with Twinkles?" she asked.

Yeah, I'd never seen him escort anyone to a seat before, either. "I think he has a sick stomach. I'm going to take him to the vet in just a second. Dante, here, was just explaining to me that there is actually something called a badge bunny. He said it was a girl who dates cops."

"Dates cops?" Kay asked and turned a look to Dante. "Why would they call her badge bunny if she dates cops?"

"Ha ha," Dante said. "I can see you two are pulling my leg." He stopped and sent a sweet smile to Kay. "Hi there. You look lovely today."

Now it was Kay's turn to blush. "Thank you. What have we got here?" Kay turned to leaf through the artwork.

Dante reached out and flipped through several of the animals. "Look at this one." He pointed to a multicolored German shepherd. "If I put a collar on him with a police badge," he spread his hands wide as if he was drawing curtains aside, "wouldn't that give a fresh new look to the place?"

"It would," I said. "But I have no money for this. Not even a dime. I'm sorry."

"But I wouldn't need to be paid. What I want to do is put it up, it won't take long, maybe a day or so. Then I'd take some pictures and try to hook into your social media vibe, include the mannequin in the pictures. It'll be a win-win. All I need is your okay. I could get this done tomorrow. Obviously, the sooner the better. People have short attention spans these days. I assume you close Sundays?"

I looked at Kay, and Kay looked at me. We both raised our brows with a private question. We both tipped our heads back and forth. We both looked down at the German shepherd, then back at each other, and smiled. I stuck my hand out to shake with Dante.

Twinkles let out a horrible rumble.

Kay put her hand on his head. "That sounds awful. Like there's a monster in him that wants to get out."

I pushed over in the booth, knowing that Kay would move with me and get up. "Time for the vet. Kay, I need to lock up and put on the alarm. How about you and Dante go hang out, get some coffee or something, and I'll call you later?" I turned to Dante. "There's a cute little coffee shop right next to the police station. They make fabulous home-made doughnuts."

CHAPTER 11

I WATCHED as Kay and Dante sauntered off. From the back, they made a cute couple. He was dark and a little roguish; she was sweet and fresh, like a bowl of strawberries and cream. If I were a writer, the sight of them might just inspire a romance novel. Maybe something about a girl traveling the world and meeting the man of her dreams. Of course, Dante walking into the picture just when I was nudging Kay and Terrance back together (where they belonged) was not great timing. I'd need to talk to her about that. A *serious* talking-to.

I sighed and looked around to tell Twinkles about it. Twinkles wasn't there. I called to him and went to search him out. He was in my office. In the brief moment he was out of my sight, he'd gobbled down his bowl of food and now lay on his back with his legs hanging open in the little stream of light that was put off by my desk lamp, like he hadn't a care in the world.

I sniffed the air to see if he'd vomited up what was bothering him, but I smelled no tell-tale signs. I was distracted from my confusion by the bell jingling as the front door opened. Shoot, I hadn't locked it.

I walked into the bar to find a woman standing next to Daphne, stroking her fingers over Daphne's cheek. A chill ran down my spine, and I patted my pocket to make sure I had my phone on me. I turned my head to see the woman's reflection in the mirror and realized she had tears running down her face. I didn't know what to do. This moment seemed brimming over with emotion for the woman, and I wondered if she was mentally stable.

I sent a quick text to Peter. **Can you swing by the bar now? Plz?**

My movements caught the woman's attention. She was trembling when she turned. I sent a quick glance to the office and Twinkles. I could see the tip of his pink tongue lolling out and that was about it. Well, surely if he thought I was in danger, he'd be here protecting me.

I walked behind the bar and picked up a cloth. "You look cold. Can I make you some coffee?"

She cleared her throat. "That would be nice. Thank you."

I watched her in the mirror as I scooped the grounds and poured the water. She ran the palms of her hands over her cheeks, wiping the tears away, then lifted a leg and slid onto the stool. I'd guess she was about mid-twenties or so. She was dressed in a pair of jeans and a rust-colored blouse that looked lovely with her auburn hair. She definitely wasn't a bag-woman or anything. If she was sliding down the mental health scale, she was a high-functioning loon. Then she went back to staring at Daphne. I've seen a lot of mannequins in my lifetime; I've never seen one that made me want to cry. Daphne seemed to be a magnet for strange characters.

After pressing the perc button, I turned back to her. "Cream? Sugar?"

"Oh, just black is fine." She folded her hands on the bar. They looked cold and bloodless. "Maybe a splash of whisky, if you don't mind."

"Irish coffee?"

"Yes, that would be nice."

When I reached for a mug, I saw the woman stroke a hand down Daphne's arm. It was similar to what the perv did last night. But not quite. It was intimate. But this woman's interaction had a forlorn quality to it. Sad. Distressed. Something about this was eerie.

"Have I seen you here before?" I asked, to get the conversation going. I had a feeling that I both wanted to hear what this woman was about to say and would regret knowing it at the same time.

"No I live in North Carolina, just over the Virginia border."

"Are you here on business?" I ran the mug under hot water to warm it, dried it off, then sprinkled brown sugar in the bottom. There's an art to making a proper Irish coffee, and if you're best friends with Connor Patrick and Mary Katherine Fitzgerald, then you'd better know the way to do it right.

"Actually, a friend of mine sent me a link to your mannequin party last night on Channel 13." She swallowed hard and glanced over at Daphne. "I came up to see Daphne for myself and to ask where you might have purchased it...her...it?" She pulled her hands back in her lap and stretched her arms out straight, locking her elbows and thrusting her shoulders up to her ears.

I picked up the coffee carafe and poured the dark roast into her mug. "I came upon the mannequin in the park. I brought it to the police's attention. They said that it would be thrown in the trash bin, so I brought it back to my bar."

Her lips tightened down to a fine, thin, colorless line. I gave her time to process that information as I poured the Irish whiskey. "Do you prefer cream or whipped cream?" I asked, trying to stay detached and professional. Which was going badly.

"Whipped, if you don't mind."

I pulled my buzzing phone from my pocket as I opened the mini-fridge and grabbed a can.

On my way. Ten minutes tops

Peter, thank goodness. I wasn't sure what was going on but I was spooked for sure. This conversation was like the shiver that runs down your body when someone walks over your grave. It was the spiders-running-across-your-scalp kind of fear. I wondered if this chick was a psycho of some kind. She held herself together, but there was an undercurrent that I couldn't define. Horror, maybe.

I shook the can as I looked toward the office door; same pink lolling tongue was visible. I walked forward to make sure Twinkles hadn't passed out or died. When I approached the door, I could see him breathing, and he popped one eye open to watch me. "Peter's on his way. Let me know when he gets here," I told Twinkles in a voice that was modulated to project so the woman knew that I had a dog and I wouldn't be alone here long.

I swirled a festive top on the woman's coffee and pushed it toward her. I looked her hard in the face, then glanced over to Daphne. Back to the woman, over to Daphne. "It's uncanny. You look so much alike. Daphne looks younger. But you two could be sisters." I scrunched the bar cloth into my hand and polished it along the counter. "Is that why your friend sent you the video, do you think? It's a very long way to drive from the North Carolina border to here just to see a mannequin. Hours."

She took a sip from her mug and set it down.

"Hot," I warned her, too late. Without fully thinking things through, I stuck out my hand. "I'm BJ Reid."

She shook my hand with ice-cold fingers. "Mary Newburg."

"Mary, this mannequin seems to be upsetting you. Do you know something about it that I don't know?"

Mary looked at Daphne for a long moment, then shook her head slowly, "No. I was hoping you knew something that I didn't." She opened her purse and pulled out an envelope. Inside was a picture that was the spitting image of Daphne, right down to the freckle on the right side of her nose. Another shiver raked over me. "That's uncanny."

Mary took a deep breath in, then let her chest fall as she exhaled. "There's a good explanation for the resemblance, I'm sure. I was thinking maybe Chloe, my sister, Chloe Walsh," she pointed to the photo, "posed for an art student. Her roommate was an art student. Or maybe she let someone take her picture." She wrapped her hands around the mug and closed her eyes. When she opened them, she said, "I was hoping to find someone who knows Chloe. I haven't seen my sister in over a year. Last May she was supposed to graduate from college. I saw her the Christmas before. Then over spring break, she disappeared. Vanished into thin air. No one has heard from her since spring break last year."

"Chloe disappeared?" I looked at Daphne for an explanation. Daphne had nothing to say on the matter. "The police didn't find anything? A clue? A reasonable explanation?"

Mary tried again for a sip of coffee; she got a glob of

whipped cream on her nose and wiped it off with her wrist. I handed her a napkin. Then, I reached under the bar and pulled out a shot glass, set it on the bar, poured Irish whiskey, and slid it to her. This woman needed something to drink, a stabilizing influence, that was for sure.

"That Christmas, Chloe had been depressed. She had fought depression since she was in high school. She was trying new meds. She was going to her therapist, but she was despondent. We were worried for her safety. We hid the guns and meds. She never talked about suicide, but her therapists had warned us to be on the lookout for signs." She stopped and cleared her throat. "My parents wanted her to take a semester off and move home. She was finishing her senior year, but when the depression hit, she didn't go to classes, didn't do her work... She's very bright. But she failed the semesters when her depression hit her hard. We had to go through letters from the doctors to get everything removed from her transcripts and so forth. My parents wasted all that money on lost tuition. Chloe was sure she could power through it through. Just one more semester. And we all reluctantly agreed."

It wasn't my time to talk. It was my time to listen. I laced my fingers and propped my elbows on the bar, then dropped my chin down to focus.

"We thought she was okay. We did." Mary nodded. "She met a guy." She chuckled without mirth. "Chloe called him her Orlando – she was an English lit major. She was in love for the first time in her life. She said she never felt so healthy and alive. Awake, she said, not alive. She was awake for the first time in her life."

The woman's complexion went grey. I was afraid she might faint. I filled the shot glass again, and she knocked it back and came up coughing.

"Did you meet this guy? Did you ever know his real name?"

"No, just that he had a gentle smile and kind eyes. We were supposed to meet him at the graduation ceremony. The whole family was travelling in."

Gentle smile and kind eyes; that could easily describe the guy who came in for a date with Daphne last night. Had he done something with the real Daphne—ehm, Chloe? What did he say he did for a living, plastics engineer? Yes, that's what he said. My lungs were tightening. My skin went cold with goose bumps. The hair over my entire body stood on end. Had I been talking to Orlando last night? Had I been in the park when he was masturbating onto the mannequin? Did he know where Chloe was? Or worse, had he done something to hurt Chloe?

I could feel bile slicking up the back of my throat. Okay, first rule in cop novels, don't jump to conclusions. Gather information. "Do you think this man has some role to play in Chloe's disappearance?"

"I have no idea. It would be nice to talk to him and ask him what he knows."

"The police haven't questioned him?"

"The police aren't really looking for Chloe. She disappeared over spring break. We knew she was traveling somewhere with him; we don't know where. She took her car, her purse, her clothes. The police think she went missing wherever she went on vacation. Or given her mental health history, that she just decided to keep going and live her life elsewhere."

"You don't agree?"

She shook her head. "When she was younger, we were very close. Depression robbed us of that same relationship. I always hoped to get it back. Through everything she was dealing with, though, we had a special bond. And something in my heart feels like that bond was broken. I just want to understand why."

"Of course you do," I agreed. "And no one has any information where she might have gone?"

"No one we can scrounge up who knew her has a clue where she could be. Her car was at the train station. The case, according to the police, is cold. They have no direction. I call them every week, but there's never anything new. And then I saw…" She lifted her hand toward Daphne and the tears spilled down her cheeks again. "I was wondering about the man standing next to the mannequin on the Internet. Terrance somebody. I thought he had a gentle smile. Nice eyes. He looked like someone my sister would call Orlando. Do you know him?"

Did I know Terrance? I knew he was over here in a hot second after I texted him the picture of Daphne. And I knew that Kay was the type of girl he liked—red-headed, slender, and with a smattering of freckles across her nose. I looked over at Daphne. Terrance and Chloe? I couldn't believe it. Besides, Terrance and Kay were in the "on" position last spring. Weren't they? I thought back to last year at this time. Yes. They were together; they went to Cancun. I hated that Mary had planted that seed in my head about Terrance being unfaithful to Kay. I'd much rather think that it was the perv.

No! Wait. I didn't have any reason to suspect anyone of doing anything wrong. Not the perv and certainly not Terrance. Okay, maybe the perv was culpable of something wrong when it came to Daphne; hard to tell. But the point here was, I was caught up in the swirl of emotion this woman had floating around her.

Chloe was probably off on some island reading great English literature with her Orlando and living happily ever after. Sooner or later she'd resurface, and this would all be a weird coincidence, because reality was, there was no reason to think anything other than that. The life-like quality of this mannequin and the resemblance it had not only to Chloe but to Kay was interesting. But I could understand why a sister would be scared for her sibling in this circumstance. I could even make a case for her four-hour trip up here to get a better look.

The bell on the front door sounded again. I looked up as Peter swaggered in. I looked back at Twinkles with a grimace. He lifted his head and gave a single bark. Yeah, great job with the security there, Twinkles.

Peter was dressed in *freshly* pressed blues with a full tool belt and a shiny badge. I blinked at the bright smile he sent me.

Mary slid from her stool. She pushed a twenty-dollar bill onto the bar and gathered her purse. "Thank you for your kindness," she said.

The move was so abrupt that as she left, my jaw hung open. The door shut and Peter was up at the bar with his hand under my chin. He gently closed my mouth and sealed it with a kiss.

"You called?"

A final shiver wrung my body. As the woman left, so too went the ominous grey cloud she had brought in with her. I focused on Peter. "I'm cold," I said. "I needed someone to warm me up."

"It's my duty to protect and serve."

"I'd like to be served now, please," I winked, and went to lock the front door. While it was true that his blue uniform and shiny badge flipped the lights on my libido, and I was happy to be serviced by Peter, why did I feel like what I really needed was to be protected? I sent Daphne a final glance to make sure she wasn't popping up out of her chair as I led Peter back to my office.

CHAPTER 12

"You're acting weird," Kay said as she tied an apron around her waist. We were opening in ten minutes.

"Yeah, I'm starting to think that we should have left Daphne in the park, or thrown her in the bin when you suggested it."

Kay moved to the cutting board and picked up a lemon and a knife. "But you did so well last night. I'm not following."

"I'm not sure I'm following, either." I was waiting for Dick to get here. He said he'd swing by on his way to his shift. Since Dick had taken the fingerprints from the mannequin, I thought I'd keep him up to date on the goings-on around her. When I told Peter after he'd shined his big gun, he was still a little too giddy to make much sense of our conversation. He kind of shook his head with a loopy smile, tucked himself back together, and headed to his cruiser for a quick recuperative nap in the police parking lot before he was called to do his sworn duty for the rest of the public.

Speak of the devil. Dick walked in with a police-blue

dress shirt and matching tie, looking crisp and sharp. He'd left his jacket in the car and his badge shined on his belt, right by his very nice assets. Yeah, I was definitely going to have to rethink my rules of engagement. Dick must have seen my eyes get all soft-focused, because he sent me a lascivious grin, stalked over, and dropped me into a kiss with a dip. I wrapped my hands around his neck and sighed.

"Yes?" he asked.

I sighed again. "I'm still deciding. This is very helpful information," I said. Not today, though. I'd already had my dose of cop for the day.

Dick righted me, but kept his hand on my waist when he turned to the mannequin. "Hi, Daphne. You changed your clothes and got cleaned up."

"That's actually what I'd like to talk to you about," I said. Dick slid onto a stool and listened to my explanation of the perv who treated Daphne as his date and the woman who came in and cried about her sister. I handed him the photo of Chloe Walsh that Mary had left behind.

"Damned," he said, holding the photo up and comparing the two.

"I know, right?"

Dick shifted the photo over to Kay. "But she also looks a lot like Kay, so it's creepy, but I don't think it's anything to worry about."

"Creepy is detective-speak to describe events like this?"

"Oh, you're asking me for detective thoughts?" He grinned, teasing me. Then the smile slid off his face, and he took my hands in his. "BJ, you know we've been friends for a long time now. And one thing I like about you is how you and your sidekick there," he tipped his head toward Kay, "seem to constantly get yourselves into the darnedest situations. Always amusing." He paused and looked me right in the eye, any levity gone. Serious. "This one's not amusing." He released one of my hands and ran his fingers through his tightly-cropped hair. "This one's got my scalp tingling."

I skipped over that last part. I'd never heard Dick say anything like that, and the heebie-jeebies I'd gotten from Mary's visit were still messing with my stomach. "Ah, so that's what you like about me, huh? That I keep life interesting." I batted my lashes, reaching for a little levity. Fun and flirty felt safer.

"Besides the obvious time we've spent together as special friends, yes, I like that about you. But let's be serious for a minute. Getting involved with missing people, especially when there are mental health issues, and the possibility for foul play is not a road that's safe for you to travel."

"So your professional take on this is that something's fishy?"

"Weird set of coincidences. I'm not a firm believer in coincidence." He slid the photo back in its envelope. "I'm going to go find out who's running the Chloe Walsh investigation and hand them this story. I'll text you the detective's name—in case they want to stop by and ask you any questions, you'll know you're talking to the right person."

"Alright."

"Other than that, I want you to stop playing with this." He pointed a finger at Daphne. "But if you want to play with a cop, I'll be happy to help you out," he said with a wink. In his eyes, there wasn't a lot of flirtation; he had actually taken on the hard edge I saw in Connor's eyes when he was in cop mode. "Seriously, BJ, consider getting rid of the mannequin."

"Okay. But I at least need it here tonight. There was a

lot of social media buzz from people on Instagram and Snapchat last night, I'm expecting another full house and I don't want people posting bad things because Daphne wasn't here."

"And then you'll get rid of her?"

"Probably. Hey, what should I do if the perv comes in for another date with Daphne tonight? Should I call the detective you're looking up?"

"On a Saturday night? I don't think they'd be jumping in a car and roaring down here. One thing we could determine, though, is if this is the guy with his fingerprints on her. If he is, then we could ask him some pointed questions about why the mannequin was in the park. If he comes in, see if you can't check his I.D. for a name and address. Maybe take a photo of it with your phone. BJ," he added, using his stern cop voice. "That's all you're to do. After that, you leave it alone. Do you hear me?"

After I agreed to his parameters, he explained how to get a good set of fingerprints. He checked his phone and shook his head. "I've got to go. Be good," he said, and leaned in for a very nice kiss (no tongue in front of Kay) and left.

Kay was standing off to the side with her arms folded over her chest. Her eyes looked ticked off. "What the heck? This sister just showed up while you were back in your office? She drove four hours to see a plastic mannequin?"

"Weird, huh?"

"I don't like you here by yourself, even if Twinkles is with you. From now on, I want the doors locked, and I want your alarm engaged."

"Yes, ma'am," I said with a little salute.

"Don't even play with me," she said, and came over to give me a hug. "I'm thinking about the sister, Mary. Until

Chloe is found, Mary's life is going to be a torment. I'm putting myself in her place thinking about you. You're the only sister I've got. What a horrible, horrible thought that you'd suddenly go missing without a clue."

CHAPTER 13

THE NIGHT WAS PUMPING. There must be something weird going on in the universe, a strange confluence of star alignments. If I knew anything at all about astrology, I'd look it up to gain some understanding. My fortune cookie at today's lunch said, "When you fall in a river, go with the flow." That seemed like reasonable advice.

At any rate, today's flow had produced a band from the local university. Just like Dante De Angelis, they hoped to coattail on Daphne's fifteen minutes of fame. They looked like they knew what they were doing. Their instrument cases were well-worn, anyway. It wasn't going to cost me anything, so why not give them a go? I moved a couple of tables out to the back by the tiki lights and let the Grork set up. I crossed my fingers and hoped for the best. If they turned out to be atrocious, I'd get Connor to flash his badge and tell them they were violating a noise ordinance or something.

The doors opened at five, as usual, but things didn't get kicking until around nine. Men in khakis and the oddly-shaped, low-slung, tapered jeans that had suddenly become a thing attempted to pick up women in summer dresses with strappy sandals. I always loved to watch that dance–so much drama, the will she/won't she? Will he/won't he. The oh-hell-no. The cat and mouse and the just plain catty. It was the best entertainment in the world to watch from a place of sobriety—how alcohol sanded down the glossy finishes and exposed the grain below.

"This band is surprisingly good," Kay said, rounding the bar and putting her tray down. She shook her shoulders and arms. "Well, you can't say anything about Hooch's being geriatric now, huh, Bobbi Jax?" Kay filled the tray again with mixed drinks and tumblers of our signature scotch.

Note to self, order more scotch. "Are people asking for the Badge Bunny Booze?"

"All I have to do is say, 'you only get to lose your cherry one thyme' with a wink and the guys are falling on themselves to order."

"Good one." We did a high five, then a down low, then we bumped butts, like we've done since second grade.

She put a pile of napkins on the tray. "Check Connor. He's giving off that cop vibe so hard, it's going to start to bring in more of his fan club. You may have a crowd of bunnies to chew on the local clover."

"More?" I asked.

Kay turned her focus toward a beautiful woman with cherry glossed lips, sucking on a Tootsie pop in the same color, like a sex kitten lapping at a saucer of cream. Her long, black, loosely-curled hair warmed her skin where her sleeveless dress left her shoulders bare. "See her?"

"Yeah, I see her," I said, with just of smidge of bitch in my voice. Look, I'm not judging her on her good taste in men. Especially men wearing badges. I guess I didn't like her doing the badge bunny hop around Conner.

"She was here last night too – in Connor's section. She's been nursing that drink for the past forty-five minutes."

"Three Coors, please." A man held up three fingers and talked over the heads of the patrons on the stools, then held out a fifty-dollar bill. I took it and rang up the order while Kay popped the tops off three bottles and handed them over. He took them in one hand, then reached for his change with the other.

I poured out some shots as I picked up the conversation up with Kay. "It's probably just one of Ashley's friends playing spy to make sure Connor doesn't stray, especially considering that they've been together this long and he hasn't put a ring on it yet."

"Don't jinx it. We don't need no bling on that girl's finger." She lifted her full tray onto her shoulder and over her head.

"Connor's decision or hers?" I followed along beside her.

"I think they both avoid that future's conversation like the plague."

"Because…"

"To be honest, I think they're just together because, well, they've always been together."

"Comfort, then?"

"Miss." A man held a finger up. "Can I place an order?"

"Be right there," I replied as I walked with Kay.

"There's nothing wrong with an old pair of comfortable jammies to pull on at the end of the day. Better than being alone," she said, then squeezed past a jumble of revelers. I headed back to the finger guy.

I hoped that that sentiment wasn't Kay talking from her own perspective. Did she feel alone since Terrance and she took this last break? My hands were working mechanically, filling orders as I contemplated how much that might play into Kay's attraction to Dante. I wished Terrance hadn't needed to leave town when he did. It would have been better if he'd been able to let things rest on the stove long enough for the pot to heat up.

I've seen it often enough here at the bar – people surrounded by people and still alone. Hmm, I'd have to ask Kay later what she was really feeling about going out with Dante. Personally, I couldn't see it. I could only see Kay with Terrance. But who was I to judge?

That was my life's philosophy, mostly. But when I looked down the bar to the woman sucking on her lollipop, I felt pretty darned judgmental. She popped her Tootsie Pop out of her mouth and used it to stir her drink. As she did that, she dipped her chin and looked up from under her false eyelashes, giving Connor a come-hither-and-let-me-lick-your-lolli stare. She popped the candy back in her mouth and looked away coquettishly. I glanced toward Connor and saw him stall as he looked over at her. Then he looked me straight in the eye and raised his brows and smirked. *Yeah, I saw her. Yeah, you're the catch of the day.* I sighed as I slid a beer to the guy on my right.

Oh ho ho! And look who was coming through the front door. It was Dapper Dan, the Pervert Man. Perv was dressed for another hot date on the town, if you were the kind of girl who went for the whole Bill Nye with a bowtie look. He headed straight over to Daphne and acted oddly enough that once again, the seat beside her was almost instantly abandoned, and he slid into his spot, reaching for Daphne's hand.

Connor came around the back of the bar and leaned down to whisper in my ear. "Looks like Daphne might get lucky tonight."

"Looks like you could, too. Let me know if you need time alone in the office with your very own representative of the Lollipop Guild."

"Aw c'mon, Bobbi Jax, don't tease. I'm sure she's a really *sweet* girl."

I swatted with a bar towel. "Connor, are you watching this?" I asked him, tipping my head toward Daphne's date.

"Yep," he said. He picked up a glass and poured off a finger of scotch. "You go take care of serving these nice people. I'll pay attention to him."

"I've got it, but thanks."

I filled one more order so I wouldn't be too obvious, then I sidled down to the perv's end of the bar. "Well, hey there," I said with a smile. "You came back."

A sweet smile slid across his lips. He ducked his head then looked up to the side to catch Daphne's gaze and back down again.

"Juliet and Romeo, right?"

"Yes," he said. "That's what I'd like."

I leaned in across the bar. "I'm checking IDs tonight," I said. "There are cops in the bar, so I'm making sure to follow the letter of the law."

He frowned at me.

"I bet you're over twenty-one." I gave him a wink. "No problem. Right?"

He pulled his wallet from his back pocket.

"If you'd like, I can run you a tab."

"Alright," he said as he drew his driver's license from a plastic sleeve.

I looked at the name and dragged my best poker face into place. I still had to turn away a bit, like I was trying to find better lighting, as I worked to hide my smirk. The perv's name was Lyle Cummings. Holy shit. How perfect was that? I couldn't wait to tell Connor and Kay.

Twenty-four, five-foot seven, a hundred and forty pounds. Huh, not an organ donor. I read over his address three times to commit it to memory. It's not bad to have a thing for numbers—I can still recall the combinations from every gym locker I've ever used

With his numbers firmly anchored in my brain, I handed the license back to him. Off to the side, just in case he came in, I had placed a glass that I had rendered finger-print-free and wrapped in a plastic bag. I used the bag to place the glass on a small serving tray. With my eye on the glass to make sure Kay and Connor didn't touch it by accident, I made up his drink. I lifted the tray and used a napkin around the glass to place it on his coaster. "Slainte!" I offered up the Irish toast.

He raised his brow.

"Health and happiness," I said as I moved away, hoping I looked casual, but really, I was quivering inside. I'd make a terrible undercover cop.

I went to the cash register, where I wrote down all the information I'd mined from Mr. Cummings's license, folded the paper, and slid it in my back pocket. My plan was on track.

"You can stop staring at him now," I whispered to Connor. "He's enjoying his date."

"I feel like I need to get them a room," he said.

"I think Mr. Cummings thinks that our dear Daphne is real."

"Mr. Cummings?" Connor's eyes lit up with amusement. "Are you making that up?"

"Lyle Cummings—it says so on his driver's license."

Connor threw his head back and laughed. He leaned in

and whispered in my ear. "I bet he got the shit beaten out of him as a kid with a name like that. He probably only feels safe when his friends are made of plastic."

"Bullying isn't a laughing matter, Connor."

"Being a perv named Cummings is."

"Stop already. Go and help out these guests. That woman over there isn't going to leave until you refill her drink."

"I think she wants to pass me her number."

"I bet it's not the only one you were offered tonight. Did the Sugar Plum Fairy hand you her digits?"

"She tried to," Connor said, filling up a stein.

"Ooo, if you go home with a napkin with a strange number and a pretty pink kiss, I bet Ashley will never let you out of the house again."

"Short leash," he said, as he pushed the beers toward the waiting hands.

"You said it," I said with a smile that I didn't feel. Connor belonged on no one's leash – short or not.

"Nah, it's not like that. She trusts me." He made the B.O. face. "Most of the time, anyway. I think my being down here at the bar is just a different situation—it seems to worry her."

"Which part?"

He turned serious eyes on me. I could see he was thinking through his answer.

"Bartender?" A man leaned forward and waved a twenty in my face.

I didn't really want Connor to answer and was happy for the interruption. Connor and Ashley's relationship was none of my business. "What can I get you, sir?" And I wasn't going to let it become my business, either.

When Lyle was nearly finished with his drink, I moved

toward Daphne's end of the bar, where I'd positioned a bowl of lemons, a knife, and a cutting board. I pulled on a pair of food prep gloves and started slicing. With his last sip, I carefully lifted the glass by the coaster at the bottom and a finger on the rim and put it down on the workspace, where I placed it in a paper bag and placed it on the shelf all the while asking, "Shall I pour you another?"

"No, I think I'm good. I must say, I really do like this place." He sent his gaze toward Daphne. "My friend here," he patted Daphne on the leg, "is such a treat. She is the perfect date."

I sent him a tight-lipped smile and moved on to ring up a tab that was being handed to me. I felt compassion for Lyle. We, all of us, are trying to live our best lives. It was sad, perhaps, that Lyle felt most comfortable in the company of a plastic doll. But look at us. Connor was dating a—well, let's be honest, a bitch. Kay was in love with Terrance, but it never seemed to work out that they were reading the same page at the same time. I... I wasn't always the girl that had played the field.

Back in high school, I'd loved a guy named Sean like my life depended on it, but then I figured out that I'm just not the kind of girl who's interested in second place. I'd made someone a priority, and I'd been only an option on his contact list. I'm a quick learner. I learned that I can have fun without the entanglements that are so painful. I didn't have to worry about bruised egos or broken spirits. Not all twenty-something-year olds had their acts together, but I'd like to think that I at least knew that I could live my life and be happy without conforming to the old tropes I saw in Disney princess movies.

I guessed Lyle and I had that in common. We were both living our truths, despite how they might be seen and perceived by the outside world. It was all good, as long as it was consensual.

I looked over at Daphne and wondered about Chloe. Was what happened last spring break consensual? Could Lyle have known Chloe?

CHAPTER 14

CONNOR DROVE KAY HOME, then me. He walked me all the way up to my apartment's door and kissed my nose, then told me to be careful and lock up tight. We had shoved the last reveler out the door at two on the dot, turned the key, punched in the alarm code, snapped off the lights, and slugged our tired butts to Connor's Jeep. And now, it was just after two-thirty.

I toed off my shoes and petted Twinkles's head before falling face first onto my bed, fully clothed. I didn't do anything to clean up the bar after the crowds finally left. I knew I'd be there all day tomorrow, because Dante would be there, sprucing up the wall. Of course, Kay planned to be at the bar tomorrow, too. She wanted to see Dante in action. It would be nice if that all worked out the way I hoped it would: a dog on the wall, some good advertising juju to pay Dante back for his talent, and Kay figuring out that Dante wasn't the guy for her, because she belonged with Terrance.

Tomorrow? What was I thinking? That was today, in just a few hours. It was Sunday already. I was supposed to go let Dante in at nine. Usually, I was off Sundays and

Mondays. Now that Hooch was gone, I'd just keep the bar closed those days. I needed to hire some staff. I couldn't keep draining Kay's and Connor's energy. They were so good to me.

I reached down to tug off my shirt when my phone rang. I picked it up with trepidation. There were no good phone calls that came in at almost three in the morning. My mind raced to thoughts of my dad. He was a fire chief. He was always in danger. And one of the biggest dangers for firemen was a heart attack stemming from all of the toxic chemicals they came into contact with on the job. I was terrified as I swiped my finger across the display. "Hello?"

"This is Shield Protection, Miss Reid?"

It was the bar's alarm company. "Yes?"

"We have activity at Hooch's. Are you inside the establishment?"

"I'm at home. Did someone break in?"

"Ma'am, there is no alarm that sounded from the entry systems. There is activity in the interior that set off the motion sensors. We turned on the remote listening, and it sounds as if someone might be in medical distress."

"Wait. Inside Hooch's? But the door didn't alarm?" Still dressed, I was reaching for my shoes.

"Our systems indicate that the door alarm was set at 2:09 a.m. No doors or windows have been accessed. At 2:39, exactly a half hour after the code was entered, the motion sensor signaled, and we listened in."

"That's so strange."

"How would you like to proceed?" the man asked.

"Could you ask the police to go and investigate? Tell them I'll meet them behind Nicky's Restaurant in the alley behind the bar and give them a key." I was fully awake now with the phone sandwiched between my chin and shoulder as I tied my shoes. "And maybe have an ambulance staged nearby just in case someone is in there and needs help?"

"Yes, ma'am, we'll contact the first responders."

I grabbed my keys and jogged toward my car. This was so weird. Could we have missed someone in the bathroom? Could someone have had too much to drink and fallen asleep under one of the booth tables? We had just kind of gathered and left. If I had been there doing cleanup, I would have mopped all the floors and seen if someone was crumpled in a shadow. *Shit. What have I done?*

I was the first one to head down the alley, but a cop car was just behind me. They turned off their blue lights as they approached. I didn't recognize this guy; he was an older generation cop with a soft stomach that muffined over the top of his tool belt, balding head, sleepy eyes. Backup was right behind him. Peter.

Peter tapped on my window, and I rolled it down. "Hey there."

"Hey, yourself. I heard the address over the radio and thought I'd do backup. Communications said they believed there might be an injured party, but the situation was unclear. An ambulance is staging at the cross street. Can you fill us in?"

I repeated the phone conversation I'd had with the alarm company. And then I told them that I had a theory that someone had been missed–maybe passed out in a corner somewhere and woken up sick.

"Obviously, we didn't see anyone when we locked up. I left the chores for today because I was beat. There were so many people here tonight that it was hard to keep track of everyone."

If I'd left someone in there, and they weren't well, would they sue me? Was this a violation of some kind? Entrapment? No, that was something else. Maybe kidnapping–false imprisonment? We had double lock bolts–you could only get them open with a key. The windows were locked too and Hooch had put some kind of film over them that made them unbreakable. In an emergency, we'd have to peel the film off before breaking the window. Was this going to get me into bigger trouble with the ABC? And most importantly, was the person okay?

I handed my keys to Peter, who handed them to the old guy. "You wait here with your window up and your door locked," Peter said. "Beep your horn if you need help."

So of course, as soon as they stacked up by the door, I jumped out to join them.

"BJ, get back in your car," Peter said.

I raised an eyebrow.

He sighed.

Old guy turned the key and pulled open the door.

Gun in hand, Peter rounded in. I waited for a split second to make sure no one fired on him, then I followed the old guy in.

We were creeping through the kitchen. Peter was using his flashlight on soft – just enough illumination to walk without tripping, still too little to drag attention to us. From cop novels, I knew he wanted to get his eyes on the unknown subject–the unsub–before the unsub got his eyes on Peter.

Kitchen, clear.

Office, clear.

Back of the bar, clear.

Definite moaning sounds. "Hey," I whispered in Peter's ear. "That doesn't sound like pain."

Peter turned toward me with "no shit?" painted across his face. We bent our knees and crouch walked behind the bar, Peter training his light at the ground. All three of us lined up behind the counter. All three of us raised up to standing. Peter flashed his light forward. All three of us dove back down and stifled laughter into our elbows.

It was Lyle Cummings living up to his family name with Daphne. He was so into it, he had no idea that he'd been spotted.

Peter leaned in to whisper in my ear. "Your call. Do I tell him to freeze or do I let him finish?"

"I'd let him finish. He'll be much more mellow a capture."

We sat on the floor twiddling our thumbs listening to Lyle's last few moments of pleasure. It was kind of a weird setup. Live perv porn isn't really my thing. If it was Peter's, he wasn't saying anything to me about it. There was no wayward hand reaching out to cop a feel. That thought made me duck my head and snicker–okay, the whole scene had me snickering.

Peter leaned in until his lips were right by my ear. "How'd he get in here?" His words tickled.

"My guess is that he wanted to spend some time with Daphne," I whispered back. "He's been here at the bar sitting next to her for the last two nights. I think he might be Daphne's owner, but when I asked, he said he saw her on social media." I waited a beat. "Surely this won't go on much longer. The alarm company started recording at 2:39. It's 3:10."

"You have to give it to the man, he has stamina," Peter said.

I wrinkled my nose. "Anyway, I think he might have hidden in the office or something and come out after we left. I bet he has no idea that he was locked in and there was no way out."

"I bet he has no idea that there are two cops here waiting to drag his ass to jail."

And with that, Lyle Cummings reached a crescendo and a finale.

The three of us rose to our feet. I flicked on the overhead light. Lyle was lying on his back his pants around his knees his trouser snake coiled and sleeping. His face was red and glistening with sweat. Daphne's tummy was glistening with – *ew!*

The old guy was the closest to the end, so he pulled the short straw and rounded the corner of the bar, handcuffs out. "Okay son, put your mouse back in the house and put your hands behind your back."

Lyle's face grew even redder. He rose to his feet, tucked himself back together, and turned around for a pat down.

"What happens now?" I asked.

"We charge him. Book him. He makes a phone call and someone comes to bail him out."

"But I have to press charges, right?"

"You don't want us to take him into custody?"

I was conflicted, to tell the truth. Mary had planted some bad seeds in my brain. I had been working those thoughts and working those thoughts and I could not, for the life of me, come up with a scenario that made any sense at all. Not a scenario that included Lyle. I didn't know that this mannequin had any direct correlation to Lyle other than what I had seen play out in front of me for the last couple of days. Lyle didn't necessarily have anything to do with the park. It could very well be that Lyle was truthful and had seen Daphne on social media, it lit his Bic, and he'd come down and acted on his personal sexual interests. I worked on my own personal sexual interests all the time.

I didn't love this scenario or the position it put me in. I'd much rather be up in my bed, mouth open, drooling on my pillow as I dreamed sweet dreams. But did the weirdness of this whole situation warrant Lyle having to pay all that money for legal help? And since he was caught in the act by two police officers and would surely be found guilty, did it warrant having his name on a sexual predator list for the rest of his life? It was a life-changing, life-destroying decision.

"Can you just get all of his information? I need to talk to Dick before I make a decision." If I gave the glass to Dick and he said that the fingerprints didn't match up, I'd just let things go and tell Lyle never to come to my bar again. If they were the fingerprints, then maybe the threat of jail would help Lyle to tell us the story behind Daphne.

"If that's what you want to do," Peter said.

"Yeah, that's what I want to do." I nodded and hoped to God I'd just made the right decision.

CHAPTER 15

Sᴜɴᴅᴀʏ ᴍᴏʀɴɪɴɢ and I was feeling like I'd been run over by a garbage truck. I didn't get home until four. Peter had followed me in his cruiser to make sure I got there safe. He walked me to my door, because he was worried that there might be lurkers somewhere that would put me in danger. Then he insisted he needed to check under my bed to see if there were any monsters. After he declared an all-clear, I got to wrestle around with his monster, after which I passed right out.

The alarm sounding at eight was torture.

TORTURE!

When did I start feeling this old? I dragged my sorry ass into the shower, into some clothes, into my car. Twinkles tinkled on the stop sign somewhere in all of that. I fed him, I'm pretty sure. But I left him at home, lest he get into Dante's paints.

When I got to the bar, I found the coffee pot was already on and there was an egg McMuffin in a bag on the counter. A note read, **Out back with Georgi, Kay.** God, I loved her.

I poured a cup of coffee and drank it down. Poured another as I looked at the note and felt guilty that I was taking advantage of our friendship. It was proving to be too much for me to work the bar, and here Connor and Kay were working two jobs. In between bites of my breakfast sandwich, I made a Help Wanted sign and posted it in the window.

Dante rapped at the front door and I went to open it for him. When he came into the bar, he did a doubletake, and then his face filled with concern. "Are you okay? You look..."

"Like shit. I'm aware." I pushed my hair out of my face. "I'm trying to revive myself with some coffee. Can I pour you a cup?"

"No, thank you. It makes me shaky. I need steady hands, or the end product will look like kindergartener did it."

I nodded and shuffled back to my stool.

"If it's okay, my car's out front and I need to unload."

"Sure," I said. "Make yourself at home."

Dante spread a tarp out, brought in his paints and brushes, and got himself settled.

The protein and caffeine both kicked in about the same time. I was starting to feel human. I guessed I should go out back and let Kay know Dante was here. And she was probably going to get a kick out of the perv story. On second thought, maybe she wouldn't. This might just upset her and make her feel like I was unsafe. I thought back to the way she hugged me after the whole Mary/Chloe event.

I opened the back door. Georgi came running over.

"If you see Kay," Georgi began, "run!"

"Why's that?" Dante asked.

I spun around; I hadn't heard him following me out.

"We're playing freeze tag, and she's it," Georgi explained.

Kay came bounding around the corner, holding her side. She hadn't run track since tenth grade, when she'd torn her ACL and ended up needing knee surgery to fix it. I didn't envy her chasing after Georgi right now, either.

"Run!" Georgi yelled. "She's gonna get you."

"Not if I get her first." Dante smiled warmly at Kay. "Hi."

"Hi yourself," Kay said.

I couldn't tell if she was blushing, or just red as a tomato from her game.

"Man, he's fast." She bent over and held on to her knees, huffing and puffing.

"Nah, you're just out of shape." I chuckled.

"Are you calling me a fatass?"

"Nope. But I am saying that even Nicky could outrun you right now."

The game over, Georgi headed back to his dad's restaurant to put the flowers in the vases for tonight's guests. Dante, Kay, and I settled in. I cleaned up behind the bar and washed the dishes. The front would have to wait until after Dante was finished—maybe even until tomorrow, when Dante said the mural would be dry enough to coat it with a protective sealant.

I went into the office to work on the accounting books. I left Kay to read a magazine in one of the booths, keeping Dante company as he worked. At lunch, they walked hand in hand down the street in search of something good to eat. I stayed back to take a nap on the office sofa, and Kay said she'd bring me some carryout.

I couldn't sleep. My mind was churning.

When Kay got back, I couldn't eat. My stomach was churning.

I was antsy. I squirmed in my seat. Kay looked over at me. "Are you okay?"

"No." I pouted.

"Maybe you need a walk around the block?" she asked.

I looked out the door, considering. "No. That's not what I need. What I need is Dick."

We both saw Dante's brows sail up to his hairline as he misunderstood.

Kay nodded serenely. "Some Dick time always makes you feel better, more relaxed. You've been under a lot of stress. You deserve it."

"Yeah, I do. Will you excuse me? I need to make a phone call."

It was a cheap thrill to watch Dante standing there with his mouth hanging half-open and his brow wrinkled. It put me in a better mood.

Back in my office, I scrolled through my contacts and tapped on Dick's icon. **Hey, there. I have a paper bag to give you and an unbelievable story to tell you. Are you around?**

Dick: **Just now waking up. Got off at 3. Heard Hooch's address over the radio. You okay?**

Aww, that was nice of him to worry. **Fine. But you'll want to hear the story. Can you come over?**

Dick: **Grabbing a shower and some grub, then I'll head your way. See you in a bit.**

It wasn't long before Dick showed up at the door. He looked

comfy in a pair of well-washed jeans and a t-shirt. He might have changed into casual clothes, but even without his uniform or detective's duds, he still wore "cop" like a second skin. It was in his eyes as he took the temperature of the occupants in the room. It was in the way he was constantly taking the pulse of the environment he was in. It was the way he tucked his chin as if coming to attention, with squared, muscular shoulders. It was in the current of authority that sizzled around him.

He pulled off his sunglasses and stuck the earpiece in the neckline of his T. I swallowed. Damn, those jeans did really nice things for his tight hips and strong thighs. Dick's gaze caught on mine and some of his sizzle arced between us. Yeah, the Dick situation needed to be re-evaluated. Just not now.

Now, my sleep-deprived brain was wrestling with logic and emotion.

"You look like you were ridden hard and put up wet," he said as he settled on my office couch.

I sent him an arched brow.

He laughed. "It was a horse analogy that didn't come out quite the way I meant it to. Sometimes I forget that you like to flavor your words with a dash of horny."

"That was poetic," I said dryly.

"What I meant was, it looks like you've had a hard couple of days, like you're not getting enough sleep. Should I be worried about you?"

"That's not the kind of relationship we have."

"It's not the kind of relationship you want with me." He settled back comfortably. "That doesn't mean that I can't be concerned about you."

I sat on the lip of my desk and put my feet in the chair. Casual. I didn't feel casual. I wasn't sure how I was feeling.

This was kind of new. "I have to admit, I haven't got my sea legs yet for being in charge of the bar without Hooch here."

"Talk to me." Cop speak. Open-ended. Let the words fall out of your mouth, and he'd piece the picture together, snag the important points and drill down.

Maybe that was just what I needed here. "Everything was fine Thursday. It feels like everything's been sliding downhill since then."

He nodded.

"Thursday I went to play in the park and found the mannequin. Hooch signed over the bar to me and took off. Nicky came in, wanting to buy me out. I promised Hooch that I would only sell to Nicky over my dead body and since I'm not especially suicidal, I turned Nicky down. He threatened me—"

"Nicky threatened you?" Dick came upright and put his forearms on his knees as he leaned forward. "How?"

"Not overtly threatened. Read-between-the-lines threatened. Something about a storm coming, and I should abandon the ship like a rat."

He nodded and went back to his slouch.

"Then I got served with ABC papers."

"I didn't know about that. What did they say?"

"A complaint about serving underage guests, and serving alcohol without a label."

"Off the record, any truth in either?"

"Our clients, the few we've had, are geriatric. Dollars to Doughnuts has been working hard to win over the police patronage. And as for the off-label, I've never seen anything. I certainly didn't serve it. Mainly, we serve beer and Badge Bunny Booze. That's pretty much it if you don't count the perv. He orders Juliet and Romeos."

"The perv," Dick said.

I pulled the paper bag from the corner of the desk and handed it over to him.

Dick opened the bag, looked inside, and rolled the top closed, then placed it on the floor beside him. "You followed my instructions?"

"To the letter. No human, other than Lyle Cummings, touched that glass."

Dick squinted at me.

"I kid you not."

"This isn't a cute little pet name, like calling me Dick instead of Richard?"

I tipped my head. "Do you feel cute when I call you Dick?"

"*Hard*ly."

Our eyes caught, and we both grinned. "Well played," I said. "But no, that is truly his name." I lifted the stapler and pulled out the tab where I had written Lyle's name and address. "But this step wasn't necessary. Peter and another cop, Joe Mannford, got hold of him last night and took down his particulars." I dove into the whole Lyle the canoodling crocodile and the roll he gave Daphne early this morning.

"You haven't been to sleep," was Dick's response. It wasn't what I thought he'd focus on. "I think you need to get rid of Daphne. She seems to be bad luck."

"Can you find out if Lyle owns one of the fingerprints? And if he does, maybe drive by his place and have a heart to heart with him?"

"He's not in jail?"

"I didn't press charges. If he's the one who took Daphne to the park, I want to know how he came to be in possession of the mannequin. Did he know Chloe Walsh? Does he know who the other set of fingerprints belongs to? I thought that having the alarm incident to hold over his head would give me some leverage."

"You probably thought right, depending on what the prints say. Go back for a second. You said, 'Did he know Chloe?' Past tense. Do you want to tell me about that?"

I looked him dead in the eye. "She feels past tense to me. And that feels pretty darned horrifying."

CHAPTER 16

I WALKED Dick to his car. He opened the door and put the bag inside, then turned to me and took my hands in his. "I'm not at work until tomorrow. I'll make that a priority on Monday."

"Thank you."

He gave me a kiss. "I'll make it a priority if..."

I looked up at him from under my lashes. A little something fluttered over my skin. If he thought I'd trade sexual favors for police action, he was sadly mistaken. And *if* he even hinted at such a thing, we'd be done talking. Forever. I'd bring the case to someone else. I held my breath.

Dick must have read something in my eyes because he looked at me quizzically. "Before I ask you what that thought was, let me finish."

I nodded.

"*If* you promise to take care of yourself. Like I said yesterday, there's no evidence that anything sinister is going down. Lyle, Chloe, Daphne, and you are probably a jumble of interesting intersections." He kissed me. "That being said, I need you to be safe. I'd rather you got rid of Daphne immediately. I'd like it even better if you gave her a social media going-away party so everyone knew you'd removed her from your vicinity. Could you do that?"

"Give her a send-off? Sure. Well, I can after Dante's done with her. The artist in there is painting the mural in exchange for doing some publicity shots that include Daphne. The bar is closed until Tuesday. I got a text that Terrance is coming back into town that morning. I could cook something up with him and take action on Tuesday."

Dick's jaw hardened.

"Not soon enough?"

"The day you found her was not soon enough. But I guess it will have to do. Now why'd you send me the stink-eye just a minute ago?"

"I had a paradigm shift. I was considering you."

"For what?"

I didn't answer.

"I swear to God, BJ, sometimes you've got me so I don't know if I'm coming or going."

I gave him a slow, sultry smile. "Oh, when I have you coming, you'll know it."

Zoom. All his blood rushed southward. He untucked his T-shirt, then put his hands on my hips, pulling me flush so I was nestled up against his high approval rating. "Will that be soon?"

"It seems things are looking up in that direction." I gave him a wink. "I need this Daphne thing to be over, and I need to get a little sleep first." What could I say? He was endearing, and loyal, and mm mmm mmm, he just exuded cop – how could a girl possibly resist?

I walked back into the cool quiet of the bar.

Dante was standing back and looking over the mural. "This isn't going to take too much longer. What do you think of it, BJ?"

"It's coming along," I said, distracted by my thoughts about what to do Tuesday, wondering if my nervous system could hold up that long.

"You're going to love it when I'm done," he said as he swished his brush in a can.

He glanced around toward Daphne. "Don't think this is weird and all, but are you playing dress-up with the mannequin or something? I could almost swear she was wearing something different the last time I was here."

I shrugged. "Every girl needs a change of outfits." I went to get myself a glass of water behind the bar. "Last night, the dress got something on it. She is the bar's star, so she has to look clean, at the very least."

"People will like that she's showing up in different outfits." He put the can down and stood to stretch his back. "Social media is a fickle crowd. They lose interest very quickly. I think the mural and pictures of her will squeak in in time, if I can take them today."

"Do you think you can finish up by today?" I looked dubiously at the wall, then down to the mockup that rested on the bar.

"I'm farther along than it looks. I'd say another hour or two and I can take the pictures. I'd like the paint to dry overnight. I can come in tomorrow morning to paint the sealant. Then you'll be good to go."

"That works. I'm closed tomorrow."

"So you're off, too?" Dante asked Kay.

"Not off-off. I'm a paralegal for a lawyers' office around the corner. I've been helping Bobbi Jax out because she needed me. But I can bring my work down here and do it over coffee."

A smile passed between them, and I didn't like it. As a matter of fact, I wanted to sabotage it. That thought and my mouth worked simultaneously. "Terrance is coming home Tuesday. I need to talk to him about Daphne."

"Terrance Pattenson, Terrance? I wondered how you got him to show up here with the whole mannequin challenge thing. He's a friend?"

I looked over at Kay with a single raised eyebrow. *Ball is in your court, chickee-doodle.*

Kay looked conflicted, and went for a change of subject rather than spell out her relationship. "Why do you need to talk to him about Daphne?" she asked me.

"She needs to go. She's pulling in a crowd that will drive away the folks I want to be the main patrons. I want the young cops to make this their go-to watering hole. A safe place to relax and be comfortable. The longer I pull in university students, the harder it will be for me to make that happen. I have my eye on the long game."

"And Terrance...?" she asked.

"Might be able to come up with some cool way to send her off. 'Bon Voyage, Daphne.' Maybe have leis and beach music. I don't know. Something. Like Dante said, the Internet crowds are fickle. I can't depend on them."

"No, but you might be able to do something like the Daphne ploy to draw in the kind of crowd you're looking for," Dante said. He walked around the end of the bar and helped himself to a glass of water. He looked over at Kay and lifted it up, asking her if she'd like some too.

Kay shook her head.

Dante moved to end of the bar and examined Daphne. He tilted his head this way and that. "The mannequin is obviously a one-of-a-kind piece of art. But the way the artist rendered her isn't that difficult. It's a mish-mash of a couple of different art classes. I'm guessing she might have been somebody's senior project up at the university."

I moved to sit on the stool next to Daphne. That was what Mary had hypothesized.

"In sculpting class, we learned how to make impressions. A simple process. You put Vaseline on someone, then take fabric strips that were dipped in plaster of Paris and layered on. If you're doing a face, you stick straws up their nose so they can breathe."

"You've done that before?" Kay asked, moving over to sit on the stool beside me.

"Sure, it's kind of Sculpting 101. After the plaster dries, you pull it off, then use that for your mold. In this case, the artist was using a porous plastic product that would allow paint to adhere. The artist then painted her using a technique called photorealism. That's why it's so damned creepy."

"It is, isn't it?" Kay lifted her lip in distaste.

Dante moved back to the sink, and with his back to us, said, "My idea was that I could make some masks for the bar." He filled his glass with water and strolled back over. "You could pick out some of the cops that you'd like to honor, and I could do masks of them. You could do a kind homage shelf."

I shook my head. "That sounds like big bucks. That's a lot of work."

Dante nodded, lifted a shoulder. "Yeah." He took a drink. "The 'oil paintings of CEOs' field is pretty crowded. I need to find a way to break out. I've been running this through my head since I saw Daphne on social media. That's actually why I came down that first night to see the mannequin up close and personal." He stopped and sent a smile toward Kay. "I'm really lucky I did."

Sap alert. Internal snicker. I looked over to catch Kay's gaze so we could share the fun, but Kay was smiling back at Dante with little hearts in her eyes. Mrph.

Dante turned his attention to me. "I thought that if I could do photoreal busts of the CEOs, that would one-up the other movers and shakers who just had the oil paintings. Everyone would be scrambling for them. After you told me about wanting to capture the cop crowd in here, I thought, you know–that might be the perfect place to start. If I had, say the chief of police, and I could show it to the mayor, the mayor would want one. If I then showed the mayor's replica to the governor, the governor would want one. If the governor had one, then it would be an easy sell to the CEOs, which is where the money is."

"Sounds like a plan," I said. "I don't see how you need me to have an homage shelf, though."

"New can feel intimidating." He cast that sentence out to Kay. "I understand that. I want to find a way to build comfort. You can't go in guns a-blazing. Sometimes it just a matter of laying the groundwork."

Kay was nodding as he spoke.

I cleared my throat.

Dante looked back at me. "I thought if I did a mask of you and Kay, that I could convince Connor to do it. If I could convince Connor, I could show that to the chief. Connor, having gone through the experience, could describe the process to the chief. From what Kay tells me of Connor, he isn't going to lay down and be incapacitated for any period of time, so I really need you," he turned his soft brown eyes on Kay, "and Kay, to try it first. To be brave enough to try."

He reached out for Kay's hand. The double entendre goopy romancy crap was getting thick. This was so out of character for Kay. Normally, this would have her in peals of laughter. But this time, she seemed to be sucking it down like a jug of water after a 10K race. Ugh.

I guessed I should have been happy for her. She looked happy.

"Are you game, Kay?" he asked.

"Sure," she said.

He turned his focus to me. "And you? Will you help me, BJ? Make a mask and tell Connor and maybe a couple of your other cop friends about the experience? Maybe we could even do their masks here at the bar, and I can buy them some Badge Bunny Booze when we're done?"

I glanced again at Kay. I didn't want to do it. I didn't want to sit still while someone draped plaster on my face. It was weird. Icky. But Kay looked blissful. And she did so much for me. She went to parks in the middle of stormy nights to bring back mannequins. She got chased down the street by a drone. She worked long, long hours here at the bar, when she absolutely didn't need the money. What was the mask in comparison to all that?

"Sure," I said. "When do you want to do it?"

"Sooner rather than later. How about tomorrow morning, I come and seal your mural? Over Kay's lunch break, we can go to my house, and I can make the imprints. It will take them some time to dry and for me to pour the medium and paint them and so forth. It's been a while since I've done something like this, so the end result might take a few days. Then, I can come and show the final project to you two and Connor."

"You can't do the masks here?" I asked, wondering how much of the day this would take, driving somewhere else. I really wanted a break—just some time to go home and lay on my couch to Netflix and chill – maybe with Dick. *Maybe*.

"If you don't mind, it really will be so much simpler at my place. I'm only ten minutes away."

"Sounds good to me," Kay said.

And I left it there. I wasn't sure this whole 'masks the CEOs' thing was going to work. But hey, who was I to naysay? Look what had happened over the last two nights because of Daphne and the Internet? I had earned enough to make bills for the next four months and enough to feel confident about hiring at least one, probably two new servers. I hoped everything went well for Dante. But I also hoped Terrance would get his butt back in town and stake his claim. Things weren't looking good for him.

CHAPTER 17

THE BAR STANK, I wasn't going to lie. A soon as Dante popped the top off the sealant lid, I got lightheaded and asthmatic. I put Twinkles on a lead, and we went for a walk. The doors were propped open, letting the air and sunlight in. Joe was back on the job, sterilizing the prep room and tut-tutting as he held up the barware I had cleaned and imagined smudges that I had left. The fumes didn't seem to bother anyone else. Hopefully, the warm breeze would clear everything out before tomorrow.

Twinkles and I went to sit at the park across from the police station, where Twinkles liked to hang with the squirrels. It was indeed a beautiful day.

You should text Kay right about now, I texted Terrance.

Terrance: **Am I forgetting a birthday? Anniversary?**

Me: **You're forgetting how good you two are together.**

Terrance: **I most certainly am not. I love Kay. Just not ready to give her a ring.**

Me: **Hmm**

Terrance: **Why should I be texting Kay?**

Me: **Because I'm a busybody who sticks her nose where it doesn't belong.**

Terrance: **Really? Shit. Understood.**

At least he was quick on the uptake.

I was feeling a weird mishmash of loyalty/disloyalty. Who was I to interfere? Maybe I should've just let Kay ride the Dante wave and see where it took her. Mm, no. It didn't feel right to me. I loved Kay; I wanted the very best for her. I thought maybe her vision was clouded. "Dante is talented. I'll give him that," I told Twinkles. Twinkles rolled over to sun his belly. He didn't seem to have an opinion.

I waited for Kay to text that Dante was finished sealing things up.

Kay: **We need to head out now to get this done in time for me to get back to work. I packed a lunch to eat in the office later. Can you follow in your car and take me back?**

Me: **Sure. What's the address?**

Kay: **2224 Whiticom Crt. Just put it in your phone. Call me if you have trouble**.

I didn't need to map it - I had a friend who used to live just off Whiticom Court when we were in high school.

Me: **Heading back now, see you at the house in a few minutes**.

No mention of Terrance. Hmmm.

I pulled up to a 1940s-style craftsman house in an older section of town. It was a lovely neighborhood with big trees and green lawns. The one at 2224 was meticulous. I didn't think I'd ever seen grass that green. I stopped to consider the house before I got out. It was obviously owned by someone artistic — the way the flower beds were laid out, the choices of color — it looked like a painting. An interesting modern sculpture stood out against the traditional lines of the architecture. It didn't clash, though; it kind of read as interesting, like wearing a pair of bright aqua pumps with a little black dress. It was all very tasteful. Kay's taste.

Something that Terrance had said by text – **I'm not ready to give her a ring** — juxtaposed with another conversation I'd had with Kay – the one about Connor and Ashley. "There's nothing wrong with an old pair of comfortable jammies to pull on at the end of the day. Better than being alone." What if the comfy jammies were packed up and flying from city to city? Then wouldn't you consider buying a new pair of jammies? A pair that had not just a house, but a home to live in? I frowned at the house. I wanted Kay to be happy. And Kay had always been happiest when she and Terrance were together. He was the yin to her yang.

Maybe I was being shortsighted. Maybe my unease with this situation was my own shit bubbling up and needing somewhere for me to project. Maybe I needed to go for a long walk and have a good think about what I wanted out of *my* relationships. Both Dick and Peter were putting out relationship vibes, like they wanted more from me than I had been offering. I had told them the deal from the beginning. They had both bought a ticket for the ride I was willing to give them. I hadn't led anyone along. I was just... tired. Confused. Overwhelmed. In a bad place. Getting my period. Needing chocolate. Lots of chocolate, and some starchy carbs.

For now, though, I could slap on a happy face, sit back, and let Kay steer the boat. I let Twinkles out of the car. "Sometimes I wish I drank," I told him, reaching for his lead. He took off running for the oak tree, lifted his leg, and marked the territory. MINE!

I expected him to run straight back to me, but his nose lifted into the air. Sniff, sniff, sniff. He followed the wind current around the side of the house, and I jogged after him. He ended up in Dante's back garden. I hoped to God this was Dante's back garden, and I hadn't made a mistake with my navigation, or I'd be explaining my presence to a cop. *Hmmm...* I thought, as a smile spread across my face.

Twinkles was being an ass. I was just going to call a spade a spade. I didn't know what got into him, but there we were, in the tranquility of Dante's backyard, and Twinkles was sniffing the ground like he was a paid truffle pig in France. Every time I reached for his lead to pull him away, he bared his teeth and growled. This doubled in strength when Dante showed up at the back door.

"Hey, what's going on?" he asked, wisely keeping the screen door shut between us.

I threw my hands in the air. "I have no idea," I said earnestly. "Just give me a second."

Kay pushed around him and came out to help me. She had a drink in her hand. I looked at it. "What is that?"

"Lemonade made with lavender simple syrup — it's delicious. Just breathing in the lavender is so relaxing."

I leaned over and sniffed her drink. It smelled like lemons and lavender. It would make a nice scented candle for a bathroom. Kay bent and patted her thigh. "Twinkle Bell, come see Auntie Kay," she crooned, in her I'm-gonna-rub-your-belly voice. It usually made Twinkles drop whatever he was doing and come running. I've even seen him drop a meat bone for that invitation. But today, not so much.

Kay looked at me and shrugged.

Twinkles started digging. Turf and dirt were flying.

"Hey, hey, hey!" Dante yelled from behind the screen door.

I lunged for the lead, wrapped it around my wrist, slung it over my shoulder, hunkered down, and towed Twinkles like a sack of bricks toward the car. He was barking his head off. I was sure the neighbors were busy quick-dialing animal control. Twinkles hadn't been himself for days now. I thought I might have read something about that in some pet magazine while I waited at the vet's, something about suddenly weird-acting pets... I tried to calculate when he'd last had his rabies shots. I was pretty sure they were up to date. Vets usually didn't let things like that lapse.

"I'm taking you home, and I'm calling the vet," I said, shoving his furry body into the back seat. I felt that had Twinkles not loved me as much as he did, he might have bitten my head off. If he was a girl dog, I'd think maybe he was premenstrual, too.

I patted over my coat pocket for my phone. No phone. Duh, I left it on my desk back when I stopped in to talk to Joe and make sure the front door was locked so the perv or another sobbing Daphne relative couldn't meander in. Tuesday couldn't come soon enough. I had texted Terrance to start coming up with a goodbye party and that's when I put it down. I thought. I hoped. Yeah, that was the last time I remembered using it... Maybe.

CHAPTER 18

I PULLED up at the front door, cracked the windows and told Twinkles to sit tight. I was exhausted from my tug of war with him. Sweaty. Rumpled. He could just stay put for a hot second. As I walked around the car, Georgi walked out of his father's restaurant. He was carrying one of the vases he'd made for the tables. He lifted his free hand about three inches and waved at me.

"Hey ho, Georgi," I said, sliding my key into the lock and swinging the door open.

"I made his for you, BJ."

"You did?" I accepted the vase. "That is so nice of you. Thank you. Can I put this on my desk so I can enjoy them?"

Georgi nodded.

I went to my office grabbed my (thank God!) phone and put the pretty aster lilies next to the lamp. I leaned out the door to tell Georgi I didn't have time to play ball with him.

"You changed Chloe's dress," Georgi said, pointing his finger.

I stopped dead in my tracks.

"What did you say, Georgi?" My heart was pounding so hard I could hardly hear myself talk.

"You changed Chloe's dress."

"I did. Yes, I did." I swallowed hard to get my saliva past the lump in my throat. "You're calling her Chloe?" How could he possibly know that name? Could Kay have said something to him? It wasn't Dishwasher-Joe. Joe had been gone when Mary was here. I was spooked, I wasn't going to lie.

"She looks just like Chloe."

"How do you know Chloe?"

"Oh, she's the nice lady on the bus. Chloe and the man. I missed my stop. I missed the red house where I was supposed to get off, and they walked me back to Dr. Baker's house to work on my speech."

This seemed wrong. "You were on a bus by yourself?"

"Yes."

Yeah, that was really wrong, Georgi should never be on a bus by himself. "Where was your dad? Why wasn't he on the bus with you?"

"Pop has a friend who is an alphabet man. He needed to talk to Pop about Hooch."

"An alphabet man? An ABC man?"

"Yes."

"But this was a long time ago?"

"Last year. A year..." He looked up. "Yes, my last birthday. Dad said I was old enough to go on the bus to the red house on my own. Watch out the window, then get off the bus and walk in the door. Only I didn't see the red house, and I got scared."

"And that's when Chloe helped you?"

"Yes. She was going to school. She was studying books.

Her friend wasn't going to school—he had a job. Like my job is putting the flowers together."

"Do you remember what his job was?"

"Taking pictures of things. He takes pictures. Do you want to play ball?" He pulled a baseball from his pocket.

"I'm so sorry. I have Twinkles in the car. I came in to get my phone." I held it up and wiggled it. "Can we play another time?"

"Yup," he said, and went out the door.

I got in my car and cranked the engine. Nope. First, I needed to let Dick know what was going on and ask him if he'd gotten anything back on the fingerprints yet.

First, I sent a girlfriend check-in text to Kay – **Snickerdoodles**

I waited.

Gr8 133m3r5 - great leemers (great lemurs). It was from a stupid inside joke we had in middle school, but we used it as code. Snickerdoodles was the "Are you okay, do I need to save you from a bad date/situation?" And great lemurs was the "A-OK, good buddy" reply. No action needed.

She was doing just fine. Good. No reason to rush back. I had time to drop Twinkles at home. I'd call the vet for an appointment on the way to pick Kay up and take her back to work. I'd just have to do the plaster thingy another day, or never. It was probably enough that Kay could describe it to Connor and the cops. I can't say that I was overly disappointed. Besides, I had other things weighing on me besides plaster of Paris on my face.

Okay, now for Dick: **Are you around? Georgi was just over at the bar and called Daphne "Chloe." How weird is that? Call me, plz.**

I looked down at my phone, willing it to ring. Instead, there was a knock on my window. I turned my head and saw the perv with a bouquet of grocery store flowers in his hands. I screamed my bloody head off.

It was just the shock of not seeing his approach and tightly strung nerves, I told myself.

Lyle went white as a ghost, his eyes stretched wide. I rolled down my window a couple inches. "Sorry about that, you startled me."

Lyle cleared his throat. "Ma'am," he said. His eyes darted everywhere, and I could tell he was having problems looking at me. I could understand that. Not so easy to look someone in the eye once that someone's listened to you during your happy time. He blinked awkwardly.

"Can I help you, Lyle?"

"You remember my name?" he asked.

"After last night, I don't think I could forget." No matter how hard I tried.

He nodded, then thrust the bouquet toward my window. "I came by to bring these to you."

I considered him for a minute, then looked back at Twinkles lying on the back seat of the car, blinking at us with his tongue hanging out. I pushed my door open, and left it open, so Twinkles could come to my rescue if perv got pervy. But I was pretty sure he was here just to apologize; I mean, his future was kind of in my hands. I decided to push forward, with or without Dick's information. I gave my phone readout another glance. Nope. Nada.

Lyle handed me the bouquet of yellow carnations. "Yellow stands for friendship, you know. After last night, and my... embarrassment, I wanted to thank you and make a friendly gesture for not pressing charges."

"You realize I haven't made up my mind yet."

Lyle's Adam's apple bobbled.

"I'm going to need you to be honest with me. I have some questions that need answers."

He cleared his throat. "I'll do what I can."

"I mean, I need you to be 'swear on the holy book' honest."

"Okay. This is about Rosebud, right?"

I tipped my head. "That's what you call the mannequin I named Daphne?"

He bobbed his head.

"I have a feeling that we met before, or rather I interrupted a date that you and Rosebud were on."

He looked at his shoes. "Yes, I'd taken her out for a park picnic." He looked back up to catch my gaze. "You see, there is something lovely about nature. The feel of the fresh grass; the sounds of nature, birds chirping, and we were having a good time, but then—"

"Then you heard a car drive up?"

"Yes, you were too close." He looked back at his shoes. "I saw a cop pull up, and I ran away. I was going to come back to get her, but my mother called, and I couldn't get her off the line. By the time I got to the park, you and your friend were tying Rosebud to the roof of your car."

"And you chased our car with a drone."

Pink rose up his cheeks until his ears turned crimson. "Yes. I know I scared you. I could see into your car with the camera. I watched you panic. I didn't mean to scare you, I just meant to follow you so I could see where Rosebud was going. And then I lost her when you were at the hospital. I flew the drone back to me and went home."

"Why did you have a drone with you?"

Lyle filled his cheeks with air until he was puffed out like a chipmunk carrying nuts back to its stash. When he released the air, he said, "The people in the high-rise apartments usually don't shut their bedroom curtains. And I like to look in."

Ew. Note to self, always close the bedroom curtains. "But you lost us. How did you find Rosebud again?"

"I'm in a group on social media–other people like me who enjoy doll-play. They were posting about her and Terrance." He gestured toward the bar. "And Hooch's."

I didn't know what to say. So I played Dick — I just listened.

"When I was younger, my older sister liked to dress me up, and she used to make me sit with her dolls. I felt safe with all of the others. They were lovely—exquisite, even. Over the years, whenever life got stressful, I'd find a doll that I could brush its hair, and that just naturally progressed. Have you ever seen something so beautiful and thought that you just had to have it – it was like life and death? Well, that was how it was for me with Rosebud. I collect mannequins, and I know to some that sounds strange, but for me, being with mannequins brings me back to my childhood. I feel calm and cared for. It's almost prayerful."

Yeah, I had heard him screaming *sweet jesus, lord have mercy,* and a few *oh god – oh god*s last night, so I could vouch for the prayer part. "I get that she is personally important to you. But I need to know where you got her." I crossed my arms over my stomach and leaned against my Mini Cooper.

"Come again?"

"She's not a doll that you can just pick up from a storefront window or in a boutique. You must have acquired her somewhere."

The crimson on his ears turned an alarming shade of

purple, he was blushing so hard. "I hate to tell you this. It makes everything so much worse. It's terrible." He shuffled his feet. "I've done something awful. Unforgiveable."

My heart was jackhammering. My blood pressure shot up so high I thought my ears would start to whistle. Had he done something to Chloe? This was my chance. I had leverage. I had to know. "Come on, Lyle, you can tell me."

He ducked his head down. "I stole her," he whispered.

The air blew out of my lungs like a balloon that had been popped. He stole her. Shit. I clapped a hand to my heart. "Where did you steal her from?"

"From the neighborhood two blocks north of mine. I was taking a stroll around Halloween, and there she was on the porch, wearing a witch's hat, sort of like Samantha on Be-Witched. She was outside, and there were others inside. They were in the window – like a display."

"I see, and you..."

"Went home. But that night, in the middle of the night, I drove over, opened my trunk, put her in, and drove off. I stole her." He bowed his head. "I'm going to jail. I understand you'll need to tell the police. It's my own fault. The weakness of my own flesh."

"Lyle, do you remember the address?" I asked gently, squeezing for all the information I could wring from him.

"Of where I found Rosebud?"

"Yes, please." I suddenly needed to pee. My nerves were doing a number on me. Now my blood had turned to ice, giving me goose bumps, making me shake. Lyle didn't seem to notice.

He turned and looked down the road. "No, I don't know the exact address. It was on Whiticom Court, and it had a sculpture in the front yard."

My eyes stretched wide. Kay! Holy crap! I snagged my

phone and dialed Kay's number. It went right to voicemail. Her phone was turned off. She would never ever, ever turn her phone off when she was with a new guy. It was against the girl-code-mutual-protection bond we'd made to each other. I jumped in my front seat, yanked my belt across my lap, cranked the car engine and took off. Lyle stood dumbfounded in my rearview mirror.

CHAPTER 19

I WAS A MESS. I was practically standing on my gas pedal, roaring down the street. I'd been parked facing the opposite direction of the police department and to be honest, in my blind panic, I forgot all about the department. I guess you could call it tunnel vision. I'd read about it in the police procedural books. It was when your mind was sharply attached to one set of information, and all other input disappeared. One cop I read about was shooting at a bad guy and the guy's partner walked up behind the cop and hit him in the head. The cop had had no idea that he was being attacked from behind. I hadn't believed it. I thought that was crazy.

You want to know about crazy? I was crazy. Kay, who looked like Chloe, was in a house with an artist who knew exactly how to make a mannequin. And Kay was alone with him. And I had to get to Kay.

Okay – I wasn't making a whole lot of sense. This wasn't making a whole lot of sense. But Daphne was attached to the house where Dante lived. Okay, people needed to know about this.

Who?

Connor.

Connor needed to know. I pressed the phone button and told the car to call Connor. Connor didn't pick up. I rambled. Screamed out some words. The address. A few expletives and a whole bunch of *now! Now! Now! Now!*

Okay, Connor may or may not get that message in time, the tiny functioning part of my brain said as my wheels screamed around a corner. "Call Dick," I yelled to my car. Dick droned on about leaving a message. I wished he'd shut the hell up and let me leave the darned message. I pushed my sweaty hair out of my face, waiting for the beep.

Beep!

Holy crap. Did I just pee on myself? I screamed equally incoherent things at Dick and gave him the address. I think I said the address a few times. Five or six times. Didn't matter. He'd need to write it down, and my words were kind of jumbling together. If I said it enough times, he'd figure it all out.

Okay, now who?

Peter.

I called Peter and again got a message. What the hell was wrong with these people? They were cops. They were supposed to come to the rescue. How could they come to the rescue if they weren't even answering their damned phones?

No. It never occurred to me even once to call 911 and besides, it didn't matter. Because here I was, jerking to a stop in front of the sculpture, in front of Dante's house.

I sucked in some air. I had to be smart about this. I opened my car door, got out, and ducked down as I shut my door quietly. Yeah, I had no idea why I was crouched like this. "Keep your head down" circulated through my thoughts, and somehow it seemed reasonable. I looked up at the house across from Dante's and saw that they had a sculpture in front of their yard as well. Sculpture – that might be a stretch. It was more like a topiary. A bush that was cut to look like a giraffe. How did I miss that before? Was that the house that Lyle meant?

I looked down the road. There were three other houses that had something in their front yards that very well could be described as a sculpture. I had lost my blooming mind. I clunked my head back against the car. *No more police novels for you, missy!* I had primed my pump with stories of the evil that lurks out there. And again, besides Lyle's theft and perversion, what exactly was I thinking happened? "Stepford Wives" flashed through my mind. But that was something about robots and ... yeah, I couldn't remember. And if Daphne/Rosebud/mannequin/big mistake did belong to Dante, why wouldn't he just ask for her back? He seemed genuinely interested in her from a marketing angle, and that was about it. And he'd moved on to a new idea.

I looked up at a woman talking on the phone and staring down at me from her upstairs window. I realized I was still crouched by my door, clinging to the handle, with Twinkles barking his head off. I stood and waved, trying to look normal. Which was, let's face it, a stretch.

I opened the back door for Twinkles, and he took off running for Dante's back yard. I ran after him. By the time I got to the back of the house, Dante was standing at the back door, with a look of amusement. "I'm assuming all didn't go as planned? Twinkles is back."

Twinkles was snuffling and digging again.

"I'm so sorry." I didn't know what to think. Dante didn't look like he'd morphed from Dr. Jekyll to Mr. Hyde. He just seemed mildly irritated that my dog was digging up his beautiful garden.

Dante opened the door. "Come on in. I have something that will make him happy." He went to the fridge. "Can I get you some of that lemonade that Kay is drinking?"

I followed him in. "Where is Kay?"

Dante pulled a steak off a plate in the fridge, opened his screen door, and called, "Twinkles, here buddy!"

Twinkles looked up, stalled, then came running. Dante backed up – as any sane person would do. That was a hundred and thirty pounds of get-out-of -my-way galloping at him. Dante moved to the side of the kitchen, opened a door, and threw the steak into the opening. Twinkles was powering ahead and chased it through the door. My hands were over my mouth; I was shrieking.

Dante slammed the door on Twinkles. Then he slammed the door to his backyard.

I backed up.

Dante stalked toward me. Walked, stalked – I don't know how to define his movements – he came forward, and I felt crazed.

"Where's Kay?" my voice quivered out. "Kay?" I yelled, backing into the dining room. "Kay?" I yelled louder, backing into the living room. "Where is she?" I asked Dante. "What have you done with Kay?"

"What are you doing?" he asked me, looking like I'd up and lost my mind. Which was feeling kind of accurate. The cogs were misaligned; things weren't working right upstairs in the old grey-matter department.

Had I lost my mind? What was happening here? Dante was dressed in a different t-shirt. He had put on cargo pants and his feet were bare. That was weirdly the detail I focused on —his bare feet.

"Where's Kay?" I swung my head around, looking for options. Maybe she was in the bathroom?

Dante held up a glass of lemonade. "Your drink?"

I blinked at him. I was so confused. I didn't know how I should be acting. What I should be doing. I wanted Twinkles up out of his basement. I wanted Connor to roar around the corner.

"Please, tell me where Kay is."

He smiled and tilted his head. "She's upstairs in the studio. She can't call down to you because she's not supposed to move her face. The plaster hasn't set."

Oh. Yeah. That was reasonable. That might be why she'd turned off her phone, too.

"Come on, I'll take you up and you can sit with her." He held his hand out to indicate the stairs, and smiled kindly.

I walked up the stairs sideways with my back to the wall. God, this felt wrong. It all felt wrong. The books all say, "Trust your instincts." "Go with your gut." My gut was telling me to smash the glass into this guy's face and run! But Kay... I could never leave with Kay in danger. I would never leave with Kay in danger. Kay, please don't be in danger.

Twinkles was going berserk. He was throwing his body against the door. I could hear him trying to get to me and that made me cry. Big gloopy hot tears ran down my face.

"You're almost there, BJ, almost there. A few more steps, and you'll see Kay."

CHAPTER 20

FINALLY, I reached studio. There was a dentist chair on the side wall, next to a wheeled trolley. The trolley was covered in a plastic bag and there was a pile of cloth strips, a bucket of grey goop, and a big jar of Vaseline. It was just as he'd described it.

There was a glass on the trolley that was empty except for a couple of melting ice cubes. I set my glass down next to it.

Kay's wrists and elbows were held in place by Velcro straps. Her face was covered in plaster, and she had two straws up her nose.

I held the back of my hand to the straws and felt warm breath coming out. But she was so still. I slid my hand in hers. "It's Bobbi Jax," I said. But she didn't squeeze back. I looked over at Dante. "What's wrong with her?"

"Nothing's wrong with her. She's perfectly fine. She said she was anxious about messing up the mask or getting claustrophobic, so I gave her a little something to sedate her so she'd sleep through the whole thing."

I focused back on the glasses.

"It blends very nicely into lemonade made with lavender. The lavender oil really helps women relax." He pointed to the glass I'd just put down.

"Women?" I choked out.

"Women," he said.

"People are going to miss Kay at work if I don't get her there in the next fifteen minutes. We're running late."

"That's true. They'll probably miss you too after a while."

I blinked.

"Things will go easier for you if you have a little drink, BJ." His smile was easy, gentle; seductive, even. "Kay would want it to be easy for you."

"What to be easy?"

"The mask." His voice was so reasonable.

He was gaslighting me. Making me feel crazy when I wasn't crazy. Something horrible was happening. I just couldn't get my brain to put it together. Where was Connor? When would Dick get here? Peter?

Dante cocked his head to the side. "You promised me I could make a mask of you?"

I swung my head around to face him. "Like you made of Chloe?"

That was the switch. I flipped it and the light came on. Dr. Jekyll slipped away, leaving a very vicious Mr. Hyde.

There. That's what I needed. Assurance that what I thought was true was indeed true. We were in danger. Big time. Kay was no help to me. I wasn't sure I could be of any help to her. The only thing that gave me even the least little glimmer of hope was imagining that one of the guys was hot on my heels coming to intervene. And should I not be able to stall that long, they'd at least have a starting point for looking for us. Or our bodies. Bodies…? "Holy shit." I stared wide eyed at Dante. "Chloe."

He lifted a brow.

"Is that what Twinkles was digging up in your garden?"

No agreement. No denial. Just eyes dark with evil and… delight.

A shiver raked over my body.

I looked down at Kay. Focused on the straws and the plaster.

"Only thing I have to do," Dante whispered. "is take these straws out and put my fingers over her nose, and she never has to wake up again." He looked at her, assessing, evaluating. "She's a beautiful creation. I am just the master to make sure that the world can appreciate her beauty."

"You're one sick prick." I reached out and yanked the straws from her nose with one hand, the other clawing at the plaster, trying to get her mouth and nostrils clear.

He was just as quick. As my hands moved over Kay's face, he locked his grip over my wrists and yanked me off-balance, stepping to the side as I skid onto the floor. I flipped onto my back and kicked out. He caught my foot and yanked me toward him. I worked to turn over and get my knees underneath me so I could push to standing.

He straddled me, wrapping my hair in his fist, and jerked my head back. Staring down into my face, he said, "Oh, this is fantastic. No one has ever fought back before. It's exhilarating. Come on, BJ, fight!" His voice was painted with excitement. Joy was the lightning flash in his black gaze.

And I did. I clawed and bit. I kicked. I hit. He was laughing. It was exhausting. His laughter was draining my strength. Anger against anger might have been easier. Laughter made me feel lame. Silly. Incapable. But every time my head swiveled and I took in Kay, I worked harder. Until he was done letting me fight. I had shoved a fingernail into his eyeball, and the game was done.

I had no idea Dante was this strong. He pushed me up against the wall, pinning me in place with his body weight, then dragged my hands behind my back.

"Where did you bury them?" I gasped. The physical fight hadn't done much. Certainly, it hadn't hurt him, or bought us much time. But when I was up against the wall, my head was turned toward the window, and I saw that Connor was here. He stopped and stared at the house, then bolted around the back. Surely he could hear Twinkles in berserker mode. I needed time. Not much. Some.

"Them?" Dante hissed.

"Lyle Cummings stole Chloe from off your porch last Halloween. He said there were others inside, displayed in the window. Chloe wasn't your only victim."

His hands encircled my throat. "I always cut off their air with the straws. But this is so much better. When I strangle you, I want you to fight hard. Fight to save your life." He laughed, and I could feel his aggression growing. "It won't help you; it'll probably make your death faster, since you're using up all your oxygen in the fight. But I can tell already how fantastic it will be."

Tension thickened the air around me. My heart beat so hard that I was sure it was visible against my shirt. My eyes welled up, blinding me. I didn't want to die like this. Would Connor get up the stairs in time to save me? Would he be calling backup? Waiting for them to come? Should I scream, or would Dante cut the sound off in his strong grip? I didn't know what to do. I didn't know... But my mouth opened, and I heard myself speak.

"Why do you do this? Do you want to be famous? Can't you do that with your normal art?" I hoped this would distract his fingers from tightening.

"Art. Ha! That just isn't in the cards. But fame, yes, that's what I want. No one remembers the good guys, the heroes. No, the people that acquire the fame are those who've left countless bodies in their wake."

"Are you trying to hurt Kay because her brother is a cop? Do you want to get caught?"

"Which serial killer wanted to get caught? All I'm doing is making the world a more beautiful place. My lovelies will live on forever. We all have to die." His words were matter-of-fact. "I'm just making sure they are plucked at the most perfect of times. Like one of the beautiful blooms in my garden."

"Your garden?" A horrible thought crossed my mind. "Your garden *is* beautiful." My voice was a mere whisper of air, barely words.

"Yes, specialized fertilizer. Lily is under my lilies. Sage is under my herbs." He chuckled. "Gloria went where I had a dead spot. I couldn't get anything to grow there–but now, it's glorious."

Oh, my god. Three more names. "Chloe is under your sidewalk?"

"Yes, well, I was having fun with the name game. I thought I would do a little mosaic up the path, like cloisonné. Now." His voice had an introspective quality, the one he used when he was talking about art and was trying out ideas. "BJ and Kay. Kay's first name is Mary. That works. Mary, Mary, quite contrary, how does your garden grow? But BJ? That's going to be a challenge.

Yeah. I promise you, I'm going to be a challenge. He was going to kill me and Kay over my dead body! Hmm, that threat didn't work, did it? "How many?" I stalled. "Where are the other mannequins?"

"Four before, six now. My mannequins are in my bedroom. They're only allowed downstairs for Halloween. We don't want to spoil them. And now they'll all have to stay locked inside, since Chloe was stolen. I need to get her back. Do you have the bar key on you?"

My mouth fell open.

"No need to tell me. I'll find it on you later."

I heard a mad scrambling on the stairs, vicious growls that vibrated through my body. Twinkles was free. Connor must have let him out. Twinkles leaped through the door and his fangs sank into Dante's arm. Twinkles dragged Dante away from me and onto the ground. He was on top of Dante, biting him. Dante was screaming. I... couldn't. I couldn't anything. Think. Move. Breathe.

I saw more movement. Flashes of blue. Men's voices. Commands. Sobbing. Oh, that was me. I was sobbing.

"Find Bobbi. Go, find Bobbi." That was Connor, commanding Twinkles. And there he was, my beautiful furball. He whined and nuzzled me, circling around, licking me, jumping up to whole-body hug me. With my arms wrapped around Twinkles, I could finally take in the room.

Connor pressed his knee into the small of Dante's back. Dante was cuffed, and bleeding profusely from his nose and arms. One eye was shut and swelling. Dick stood over Kay, checking her breathing and her pulse. He picked up a cloth and wiped the last of the plaster off her face, then patted her cheeks, trying to rouse her.

Peter came in and took hold of Dante, wrangling him to the corner and reading him his rights. Connor checked Kay for himself, then pushed Twinkles down from off me. Connor was probably the only person in this world at that moment that Twinkles would allow near me. Connor reached out to pull me into a hug of his own. I could feel him trembling.

"Oh, thank god," he said into my hair. "I heard your voice on my phone and terror–that's the only possible word for it. The two women I love the most in this world..."

He didn't add anything to that sentence, just held me tight as he spun me around so he could watch Dick talking to Kay. She was awake and looking around as Dick explained the situation to her.

I pointed toward the glass on the tray. "They might be able to test that glass for whatever he used to put Kay out." It was the first clear thought I'd formed since I was talking to Lyle.

Connor dropped a kiss into my hair. My cheek rested against his chest, and I could hear his heart galloping. His phone rang with "Million Dollar Baby." I glanced up to see Connor make the B.O. face. He swiped the screen to stop the noise.

Shit.

Shit. Shit. Shit.

A serial killer, Dante had said. We were on his list. We survived.

And to think, this all started with a mannequin and a little afternoon of sport.

Kay looked over at me, looking a little drunk. She giggled behind her hand. "Bobbi Jax," she snorted, "looks like I got to see how you can make three cops come all at the same time."

I winked at her. "Just one of my many talents."

My other talent was one we shared – finding ourselves in the middle of crazy situations. The ambulance had brought a gurney up for Kay. I needed to get back to the bar. I could hear a shot of Badge Bunny Booze calling my name.

THE SERIES CONTINUES ...

IF YOU SEE KAY HIDE

It's not every day that Twinkles poops glitter and jewels. It's almost like I have my very own Golden Goose. Has my world changed from bar rags to riches?

Also by Fiona:

The Lynx Series
That Which is Yours
Weakest Lynx
Missing Lynx
Chain Lynx
Cuff Lynx

Strike Force
In Too DEEP
JACK Be Quick

Uncommon Enemies
WASP
RELIC
DEADLOCK

Kate Hamilton Mysteries

Mine
Yours

Also by Tina:

Spark Before Dying Series
Deadly Sins
Angels Cry
Burden of Proof

Det. Damien Scott Series
When the Devil Takes Hold
Sticks & Stones
Foul Play

Glasneck & Quinn - Brew Ho Ho

Connect with Fiona Quinn at www.FionaQuinnBooks.com
Also:
@FionaQuinnBooks on Twitter
Fiona Quinn Books on Facebook
Fiona Quinn Books on Pinterest

Connect with Tina Glasneck:
I enjoy connecting with my readers. Send me an email,Tina@TinaGlasneck [dot] com, and I promise to respond!

Join my newsletter, connect with me on Facebook, and never miss a release, as well!

DID YOU ENJOY IF YOU SEE KAY RUN?

Recommend it:

Please help others find this great story by recommending it. You can also recommend it by posting about it on your social media sites, like Twitter and Facebook.

Review it:

Please tell others why you liked this book. You can review it where books are sold, and in your online reading communities.

ACKNOWLEDGMENTS

We'd like to acknowledge our editor, Lindsay Smith, and our cover artist Chandell Aikman Sites, for their hard work, dedication, and professionalism. Thank you ladies for helping to make this jewel shine.

To our beta readers and our street team members, thank you for your support, enthusiasm, and excellent feedback. And Sisters in Crime – Central Virginia for introducing us.

To all the wonderful professionals who helped us get the details right, especially our local law enforcement, who provided the Citizen's Police Academy. Please note in fiction, while we try our best to get the details right, we have not committed any crimes, so in the end we had to make some stuff up. Please understand that any discrepancies come from our authorial decision making, and rest squarely on our shoulders.

We'd especially like to thank Hardywood Park Craft Brewery, and the Brew Ho Ho event for providing us with the excellent beer fumes that inspired this series.

Thank you to our husbands because they are fabulousity personified.

78429552R00100

Made in the USA
Columbia, SC
16 October 2017